HOMETOWN BREW

HOMETOWN BREW

A novel by

ELLEN AKINS

Alfred A. Knopf *New York 1998*

This Is a Borzoi Book Published by Alfred A. Knopf, Inc.

Copyright © 1998 by Ellen Akins

www.randomhouse.com

Library of Congress Cataloging-in-Publication Data
Akins, Ellen.
Hometown brew / by Ellen Akins. — 1st ed.
    p.   cm.
ISBN 0-679-44795-4
I. Title.
PS3551.K54H67   1998
813'.54 — dc21   97-49477   CIP

Manufactured in the United States of America
First Edition

To Steve,
in case one that really
suits you never comes along

PART ONE

I

Alice at seventeen had posed for some pictures that made their way into a men's magazine. At the time no one would have believed it, because she was a shy and serious girl, awkward with boys and of not much interest to them, as her beauty wasn't the assertive sort and she didn't have the personality to make the most of it or to make herself desirable without it. She did, however, wish to be desirable; so, when a man presenting himself as an artist asked to photograph her, she was more pleased than skeptical. What he said was what her mother often said—that she was beautiful in a way that took some looking to see—and it occurred to her that an artist might be able to reveal enough of this alleged beauty that some of the looking it required could be skipped. Then the nature of the pictures he wanted to take became apparent, and she discovered the possibility of a sort of beauty in herself that her mother wouldn't know about, and she did what the man asked. Although he didn't touch her, this was her first sexual experience. As she took the photographer's directions, reclining with her hands in her hair or lying on her belly with her underpants pulled down, she felt herself being admired by a whole anonymous audience of men who normally wouldn't have noticed her, and this secret power thrilled her more than the most adept touch might have. In a purely practical sense, this sensation required the presence of the man taking her picture, and yet he might as well not have been there.

She didn't know anything about the disposition of those

pictures until a boy in the junior class confronted her with the magazine in which they'd been reproduced. Looks just like you, he said, very pleased with his discovery, and her dismay was such that her dismissal of the resemblance—and of the boy as well—carried conviction. He was no one she would have imagined looking at her, though she could easily have imagined him poring over the magazine in question, in which hers was the most modest appearance—as she was at leisure to discover, since he tucked it into her book bag.

The boy—once called Little Joe to distinguish him from his father, and now called simply Little, although he was anything but—did believe her. He did believe that he'd only imagined that this girl was Alice; but by showing her the pictures, he'd brought her into his imagining, and thus established an intimacy between them. What followed for a few years then was a tenuous relationship of pointed teasing on his part and prickly indifference on hers, until at last Little's chances of moving beyond pictures improved, other women came to occupy his mind and energy, and he began to leave Alice alone. Eventually his thoughts about her, touched and retouched over time, were as soft in focus as those photographs that, it seemed in the retouching, had shown him his first love.

2

Close to when Alice was having her picture taken, one of her fellow townspeople, Melissa Johnson, herself nineteen and no more worldly or wise, was in the throes of giving birth. A privileged life had given her a notion of trouble as something that couldn't last, that, in the rush of events in the other, felicitous direction, would always have to give. It was a notion that could hardly survive the long trial of labor, let alone the longer sense of consequence that shadowed the baby into the world. But coming as this reckoning did at the end of the ordeal, it got turned around too, overwhelmed with relief, and Melissa for the moment was more aware of having survived than of having changed.

She had been at school in Boulder and had stayed there in the naïve belief that she could keep her predicament from her father, who stood at her side now, precisely where his son-in-law might have stood had there been one. When the pain suddenly ceased and a peace almost psychedelic in its clarity settled on her, she observed her father holding out his hands like a celebrant at mass. The doctor, either not seeing or not caring, lifted the baby over her sagging knees and laid him on her chest. It was a minute before she could raise her eyes from the tiny, mewling creature, and then she saw, or later remembered seeing, her father with his hands still outstretched and, for the least instant, a loose look of wonder on his face, as if a magic trick had just been practiced on him. As soon as she noticed this, it disappeared and he was slowly lowering one hand to administer the most reverent touch of a fingertip to his grandson's back. His expression was infused with pride, or seemed to be, though at the moment she could hardly distinguish what she was seeing from what she was feeling. Later she associated the surcease of pain, the very moment of Jesse's birth, with the sudden end of every other kind of pain the baby's coming had caused, every unsaid question and concern and disappointment.

This was the end of her schooling. Her father took her and the baby home to Rensselaer, where, to her surprise, her brother, Frank, who'd been serving a year-long apprenticeship in a brewery in Munich, was waiting to meet his nephew. Not quite eighteen, Frank had already completed his studies at St. Paul's, a preparatory school in New Hampshire, worked a summer for their father, and spent seven months in Munich. He'd been his sister's first baby, a sweet and needy playmate for a little girl, but in the ensuing years something had happened to him, a tempering process more than any particular event, through which he had come to seem not just older than Melissa but sometimes a stranger to her. He was a boy who knew his mind insofar as it was directed toward a certain object, whereas she was not so certain, and not so certain which was the better approach.

Now, though, when Frank gingerly took the baby from her and, looking stricken and gifted at once, cradled him not quite against his chest, there was none of that pinched, reprimanding oldness about him. What she saw instead, with what she assumed was the newly mature vision of a mother, was the old childish neediness and desperation. At the moment she was especially susceptible to such a picture, and her sudden affection, constricted so long, overwhelmed some sensible reservations. They made a charming picture, her fair brother and her fair little son, and if anyone had looked in on the lot of them, her fair father as well, she, with her mother's olive skin and dark hair, would have looked like the interloper among them.

Their mother, dead three years now, had been Spanish, as

people imagined they could tell from her inflections and gestures, when, the truth was, deprived of her dark appearance, they could not have told what climate, let alone what continent, produced her. Melissa, even less the exotic in taste and temperament, had inherited the misleading look, while her brother, as outwardly Nordic as their father and every other member of the family as far back as records went, seemed to harbor the passion of their mother's nature, and harbor it much as their mother had, secret and banked, only scintillating now and then in the fierceness of its restraint. This was as much as mother and son had to do with each other once the romance of childhood was over.

It was perhaps odd but no less sweet that Melissa's motherhood took the two of them back to their childhood. For a while they were once again contented children in their father's house, no more concerned than the baby about worldly business. This was more the case for Melissa than Frank, since from the very onset of her pregnancy she'd felt herself softening, submitting happily, helplessly to her transformation, and since she could think back to all the books she'd read as a girl, in which children were motherless, as she was now. That, the missing mother, was somehow the secret garden as, surrounded by the trailing plants and small potted trees in the conservatory, she dreamed her way back into those stories, velvet rooms and cold attics, she'd inhabited more than read. Sitting in the sunny room, nursing the baby in a sensuous stupor, she raised her eyes to find Frank standing at the glass door, so intent that it was a second or so before he noticed her looking. Wasn't it funny, she remarked, in an attempt to put him at ease, that a breast put to its intended use lost its significance, wasn't a *breast*—that she could just go out in public like this?

This wasn't public, he was quick to inform her—and then to add that, if he were her, were a girl, he would cover himself, as she was now.

When she was done, he wanted to know, could he hold

him? He hadn't much time left for playing uncle, since he was going back soon. This was the first she'd heard of his going, though it wasn't surprising, less so in fact than his coming had been. Within a week he was gone.

What she herself would do next was the one matter of contention between her and her father. She'd gotten into a policy of agreeing with him, because he was forceful and generally right, and because what he wanted was usually to her advantage, but the luxury of home, with a maid and cook and gardener-driver to do the things that she'd ineptly done for herself for two years or so before moving back, finally reached surfeit with her. She missed the luxury of her ineptitude—the unjudging solitude, wearing pajamas and robe till noon without feeling indulged by anybody but herself, making macaroni and cheese at whatever the hour and calling it a meal, watching TV if she wanted. And despite what people said about a boy needing a man around, she didn't think her son needed a model quite as compelling as her father quite so close.

He had been insisting that the young man, as he invariably called the baby's father, be persuaded—paid, if need be—to sign a disclaimer waiving any right to see his son in return for freedom from any obligation. Now she had no wish to see Jim, whose attraction had disappeared promptly with her period, but she didn't want to rule him out entirely either, in case Jesse someday wanted to know him; and, finally, the idea of using money to get something out of him was, in view of all they had, a little sickening, especially since her father meant to relieve Jim of a burden that he himself wanted more than anything to bear. She said it might be best if she just moved to Colorado, where Jesse could have the benefit of both parents—which, though it was only bluff, suddenly induced her father to see the sense of her wanting a separate place, if only across town. The disclaimer was not mentioned again, except once by Curtis Niemand, her father's lawyer and friend, who evidently hadn't been brought up to date, and who, after a second or so of confusion that she explained away, retreated, begging pardon. The troubled way he considered her, a bit like her brother, made her feel a little tender toward him, and she found she didn't mind being the cause of his discomfiture.

For the square, two-story house that she and Jesse eventually moved into, her father paid, about which Melissa thought, on those rare occasions when she thought about it: Why not? He was as rich as all hell and he loved her.

3

It was some years later and not long ago that Alice Reinhart once again appeared in Little's sights, though this was not her intention. Her fortunes were also founded on the doting of an older man, but one without much of the fatherly about him, and after thirteen years in thrall she had fled him for the only other notion of home she had, the place she'd come from, which once had seemed its only virtue.

The first time Little saw her again he didn't know it. At a distance of not quite two blocks, she appeared as a stranger on his street, emerging from a house that had been vacant for months and turning down the sidewalk toward town, away from him. Something in her carriage, a certain easy indifference, suggested youth and beauty, which at once aroused his interest and warned him off. Two days passed before he turned a corner at work and found himself face to face with Alice, whose hair, a long and coppery auburn now, identified her as his new neighbor. There was nothing subtle about her loveliness anymore, and that sweet, anxious quality that once disarmed his awkwardness had disappeared into a look of waiting, with some expectation in it. Facing her that first time, he felt as if she'd asked him a question, though neither had spoken.

"Speak of the devil," he said, for lack of any other words; for as little reason, Alice laughed. He was so struck by the sight of her, his smile was slow to follow. He'd heard that she'd been living in New York with Alex Saxonberg, an old man

from Rensselaer who'd made his money running "art" the-
aters and adult video stores across the Midwest, and it was to
this doubly alien circumstance that he attributed the strangeness of her looks, which were unmistakably Alice Reinhart's
but different enough that he had to assume she'd done something with makeup. Trying not to stare, he'd fixed his gaze on
the artfully darkened corner of her eye when she said,
"Wouldn't it be fun to have a beer?" the wistfulness of it suggesting that they were in a desert or a monastery, not a brewery in the middle of Wisconsin.

He didn't see her again until they met on the steps at the
end of his shift, and this time she was wearing a Gutenbier
uniform. A blousy navy-blue jumpsuit with the book-and-
bottle insignia on the breast, it looked more like a costume,
since otherwise there wasn't a sign of work about her. "You
don't have to wear that out," he said.

She said, "I just put it on."

As they walked, he imagined himself at eighteen witnessing
this scene, Little Martin escorting Alice Reinhart to a bar at
her request, and the unlikeliness of it sobered him somewhat.
There had been nothing suggestive in her invitation, no matter how he scrutinized it. Alice apparently had gone so far
past him that not only was he not worth avoiding anymore; he
might be an innocuous diversion.

In this capacity, Little whiled away a good ten minutes relating anecdotes about the brewery. He knew, for instance,
that the man who'd started the company at or around the turn
of the century was named Johnson, like so many other people
in the town and elsewhere that he'd wanted something different for his beer; also, something German, because the Germans made good beer but, more than that, because they
drank it and were even more plentiful here than Johnsons.
And so, between the dictionary and the Bible, Johnson had
come up with Gutenbier.

Alice repeated it softly, lingered over the word as if she

were tasting it. "My name's German," she said, then added for clarification, "Reinhart." Everything she said, barely above a murmur, seemed a confidence. The way she listened was intimate too, her dark eyes wide and so slow to blink that she might have been spellbound, her lips parted slightly, the pouty lower one rolled out a little, giving her that languorous look he'd seen on so many models in *Penthouse*; if he hadn't known better, he would've thought she was trying to seduce him. "And they still own it," she suggested.

"Gutenbier?" he said. "The Johnsons? That they do."

"I know," she said. "I met the one."

"The old man?"

"No, young."

"Oh, him."

" 'Him,' the way you say it, what?"

"Did I? I didn't mean anything by it. I don't really know the guy." For a few seconds they looked at each other as if a curious fact had just surfaced. Then Little tilted his bottle to the light, gauging how much was left, and asked her what brought her back to Rensselaer. "Not a job at the brewery, my guess is," he said.

"I can tell you," she said, leaning a little closer. "I left my husband. You probably know him, know about him, I mean—Alex Saxonberg?"

He said, "I didn't know."

"I thought everybody knew." Her confidence, *I can tell you*, had opened up for him a view of her life as so friendless that someone like him, a near-stranger by now, might be the closest anyone came, and he found himself beginning to feel protective about her again.

"I was married too," he said. "Things happen."

"But that's what I wanted," she said. "Things to happen. I used to. That's why I got married, or why I got—you don't know who Alex is?"

He expected her to tell him something then, as women

tended to do whenever he made simple statements that implied a great deal. It was his concession to the complexities of life, all those things that he thought a person ought to acknowledge but probably shouldn't attempt to discuss, since they had a way of changing with wording, getting that much more complicated and incomprehensible while you thought you were making some sort of sense of them. In his experience, all he had to do was hint at the intricacies and a woman would start to unravel her own. It was, he thought, like meeting a foreigner and saying some small thing in her language to make her feel comfortable and releasing from her a whole burst of foreign words that he couldn't really understand but she believed he could. However, this didn't happen with Alice. "It's complicated," she said softly, after some thought. "But not anymore. Not for me. I'm all through with complications."

Little said, "That's good to know."

Briefly, in that caressing way Alice regarded him there was a hint of condescension. After all those years of drifting, she imagined herself at a worldly distance from what was visible, palpable, the fleshy self that she'd left with Alex because it seemed entirely his idea. Worldliness was thus precisely what her past had spared her, and what went by that name for her was not much different from the unworldliness of ascetics, for whom physical nature, though so beside the point, still perpetually required being put in its place with a lash or a chain or a diet of worms.

4

Word hadn't yet reached the workers that Gutenbier had recently undergone a significant change. There had been a fire at the brewery, as was well known to all, followed by shifts in management within the Johnson family. These were so long expected and unremarkable in view of Mr. Johnson's age that they aroused the sort of interest and comment generally associated with the weather, whose operations were as distant and effects as immediate as the doings in the upper reaches of the Johnson family.

It was in the nature of the brewing business—small as this one was, with no reserves of cash to speak of—that Gutenbier depended each year on a loan that bought the supplies, from malt to hops, that made the beer that paid the loan off later, and for as long as anyone could remember, the banking concern that conducted most of the town's financial business had managed this business as well. Gutenbier was a good part of Rensselaer's economic backbone, and brewing and banking had always worked well and smoothly together in this circular arrangement. But now, when Mr. Johnson put together his plan for rebuilding and expanding the part of the plant damaged in the fire, the bankers demurred. The plan, they said, would not simply freeze in place but amplify a system quickly growing outdated in the face of technical advances in the industry.

That Gutenbier was as much a tradition as a business made little if any impression on the bankers, who preferred a tradition with a few anachronisms to a dead one, which was what they foresaw. That Gutenbier could end its long-standing relationship with these men and find others more amenable wasn't likely, because what was suddenly objectionable in them was, as Mr. Johnson knew, a widespread phenomenon he'd only managed to escape till now through these very men's own anachronistic practices. Furthermore, what they were proposing was hardly radical: Since he clearly wanted to keep the brewery in the family, why not delegate more of the running of the business to his children now? Hadn't he been grooming them for just such a move? Why not install Frank? Or establish a voting trust, with Frank and Melissa and himself as members—Curtis Niemand too, if he liked—and conduct the transition himself?

Presented by her father at a board meeting as an unavoidable circumstance of doing business nowadays, this news nonplussed Melissa; the larkiness of his announcement, frustrating further inquiry, made it even stranger. She pressed him, but he wouldn't be held to the subject, and finally, dogged too far, he spoke her name in the basso profundo he reserved for the rare rebuke. She was already feeling chastened when he asked her, requiring no answer, "Have I ever failed you?"

Comforting as it might have been that he was still very much himself, this didn't make the situation any less baffling. Her father was old-fashioned, but not particularly old; he knew the business better than anyone. For the bankers to imagine any benefit from easing him out, especially in favor of Frank or a neophyte like herself, was so unlikely from businessmen normally so deferential to her father, that she had to assume there was some obscure sense to it, and when it didn't come clear under further scrutiny, she finally went to see Harold Young, president of M & A Bank.

He asked her if her father knew she'd come to see him. She said no, and he nodded as if to say: You see?

"There have been a few incidents," the man said at last, "but of a personal nature."

"Incidents?" she said, and with tilted head and tight-lipped smile, he raised his hands in reluctant concession. When he'd gotten the better of his scruples, he said, "Of course you know he tried to change his name."

As coolly as she could she said, "That's an incident?"

"It suggests a state of mind."

Again he struggled with his conscience, his working lips the salient—and again they gave. "I don't know how many confidences I'm betraying if I mention a Miss Lowell."

"Annie?"

"Yes, I understand she was engaged to your brother."

"She was. She isn't anymore."

"And you know the circumstances behind that?"

"That? You mean the breakup?"

"The breakup. I suggest you ask your brother—if you really feel compelled—but I can tell you this much. It's a piece of luck you didn't learn about it from the paper."

"It's strange enough to hear about it from the president of the bank."

Knowing as little as she apparently did, she didn't know what to say next. Mr. Young spared her the effort. "As I said, personal, and I'd just as soon leave it at that, but put alongside a few of his recent decisions. That proposal of Frank's, for instance. And now his plans for restructuring—if they weren't so ill-advised, I'm sure you'll agree, none of this would've mattered, but the long and short of it is, we just don't know that he's up to it. That may seem hard—but it's a lot of people's money we're working with here, every small investor and depositor, so it's critical that we err on the side of caution. If it were my own money . . . " He shrugged, helpless.

"Yes?"

"Of course I'd do it in a minute."

"You mean you'd do differently with your money than with your depositors'? Mine, for instance?"

He seemed not to understand the question, and immediately she felt ridiculous: of course he would, in a minute.

"What everything comes down to," the man said, "is what's the best for Gutenbier. I'd like to think that would be his first concern too, but again—"

"It is," she said. "I'm sure of that. But his idea of what's best for Gutenbier might not be the same as yours, and he's the one who's been running the brewery for almost thirty years."

Her idea of what was best was not an issue, she was a bit offended to note, and a bit relieved too. Even so, Young and his cronies were prepared to put a third of the authority over Gutenbier into her hands—although, in view of the impression she'd probably just made, it was hardly likely that she'd ever see that kind of power, but who was he to say? A gossip, and what really irked her was the man's presumption, not so much in speaking of these private matters but in knowing more about them than she did. Her father had tried to change his name? It made no sense, and not just because what he tried he always accomplished.

When she got home, she found her father's gardener mowing her lawn. Her surprise was uneasy in a way it might not have been two hours earlier. To send Abel to mow her lawn was not outrageous, was in fact just like her father. Once, not all that long ago, he had dispatched his maid to take in the laundry she'd hung out to dry, which was like him too but a bit odder, and eccentricity was, after all, a matter of degree. It was also possible that she was the odd one, since this had happened in the winter and the maid, Mrs. Carpenter, had seemed more puzzled than dismayed to inform her that the wash had frozen.

Now she called across the lawn, over the mower, "I was waiting for the daffodil leaves to die!" but Abel merely flapped his hand at her, and because he was the one who'd taught her the little she knew about gardening, she left it at that. The scene was so summery, the smell of the cut grass so sweet, that she stayed for a minute breathing it in.

She and Jesse were having dinner at her father's—to collect them had been part of Abel's mission, which meant the three of them sitting close in the cab of his pickup, a prospect that always led to a last-minute scramble over seating as Jesse maneuvered himself next to the window. He was a little shy of brawn. This time, though, he climbed in first, quickly, and sat through the ride harking head to toe, never quite looking at Abel but not really looking anywhere else. Melissa sympathized, since the man's bluff, blond good looks and rough charm and size, too much like Jesse's father's, intimidated her as well, but when she squeezed her son's knee he shrank from her, pressed closer to Abel, and it was all too strange.

Her father, their host, was not home. As she stood on the porch, wondering whether to start or to wait, a car turned in at the gate, but it was only Curtis Niemand's silver Lexus.

"Are you coming to dinner?" she called when he opened his door.

"Let me guess," he said, strolling toward her. "He's not here."

"Has he done this before?"

"To me. Not to you?"

"Not so far. So what do you do? Stick around?"

"For a while. And he usually shows up."

She stood for a minute thinking, brushing her hand with the end of her braid, while Curtis watched her face.

"Is Frank coming?" she asked him.

"My guess would be no."

She sighed, and he smiled, and they sat down on the wooden chairs on the porch. Frank wasn't often invited to dinner, because, as her father had explained, all he ever seemed to talk about was work, which was a good part of what made her feel bad. Even now she knew she could safely bet that her brother was still at the brewery, where, it was true, he would just as soon be, but that hardly made her feel better. In one way or another her brother was always at work, was, though younger, far better prepared and more eager to protect the family's interests, while she, who'd been feckless and had to be nearly coerced into going to work at the brewery, enjoyed her father's favor. It was the peculiar curse of the prodigal son that as much as she frittered and wasted came back to her in the way of happy returns while Frank, whose life was one long wise investment, didn't merit so much as a fair share of interest.

"He's probably at the office," she said to Curtis, who, with no more than a quirk of the brow, managed to convey a shrug.

"Someone has to mind the store," he said.

She said, "Why?"

"Well, I'm glad to see you've put aside your socialist tendencies for something practical, like anarchism."

She laughed. "I mean now. Nobody has to mind the store now. You know, he's just trying to make the rest of us look bad. I wish he would take a vacation." At once she rethought this. "Maybe not. Curtis, can I ask you something? About my father. It's personal, but—"

He raised his palm as if protesting or taking an oath.

"OK, it's this. Did he try to change his name? That you know of?"

His upright hand lowered to wrap itself around his chin, and he studied her. "You know your father at least as well as I do," he said at last. "If he wanted to be called something else, can you think of anything that would stop him? Short of main force?

"So he's getting older, having mortal feelings—it's hardly surprising—and in this case, just for a moment, those feelings focused on Gutenbier. first the fire, then the bank, and who knows what else—it's been enough to make anyone worry. So he decided to link the family and the brewery in what seemed, *for a moment*, a clear and irrevocable way."

"I'm sorry. I must be missing something."

"He considered changing his name to Guten."

Not knowing how to react, Melissa said, "Oh." Then, "Guten." And then, "His last name." Curtis nodded, as if now everything were clear. But this was clearly more than a minute's mania, if it had gotten far enough to figure in Mr. Young's calculations, and she was framing her next question when Mrs. Carpenter opened the door and asked her to come to the telephone.

It didn't strike her as odd right away that her friend Sue, who had only to say, "Thank God you're there!" to make herself known, should be calling her at her father's house. Her concern simply moved from her father to Sue—so, when her friend said, "Your dad," that seemed natural too.

"He's not here."

"I *know*," Sue wailed at her, "Me*lis*sa. He's *here*. I think he's having a stroke."

5

In the darkened Gutenbier building on the edge of downtown Rensselaer, in the offices that anchored the brewery's bottle house, Frank Johnson was still at work. Work for him was not what it was for his sister; it was the name he gave what he preferred to do, and by night, in those hours that gave him a sense of having the world to himself, it was particularly sweet.

In the circle of light cast by his desk lamp he bowed his head over an array of advertisements featuring women: a topless model hugging her blue jeans; a skier sporting nothing but boots; an orgy of bare bodies inspired by the perfume pictured in the corner of the page; a woman embracing a bottle of whiskey (or maybe riding it); and one photograph after another of curvaceous blondes in tiny bikinis, arriving via parachute, roller skates, or water skis with a supply of a competitor's beer for a few thirsty young men. It might have been another species he was studying, he looked at the pictures so curiously. Then he shifted to the storyboard that Dunwitty & Howard, a firm out of Milwaukee, had drawn up for him. The storyboard was too sketchy to offer a reliable comparison, but Frank suspected he would do no better with a polished piece of work. He had no way of judging what was good, since what he wanted from these women wasn't what he was supposed to want, what made their images work on men. He wanted what they represented, because they *had* worked, and thus he viewed the *Playboy* laid on the corner of his desk, in which the blondes were liberated from their bikinis, as the ultimate prize—proof that advertising could move from its medium into the culture at large, presumably taking its product with it. But, then, he had to wonder, had it? Was the name of the beer on the lips of the men who pored over these pictures, as it was on his, or had the women obliterated the last least trace of it? He *was* aware of wanting a beer, but he could hardly credit the ad for that.

His own tastes weren't a proper measure for the enterprise. Solicited like this, his longing was analytical, his appetite working out the calculations of anyone trying to pique it, so that each woman on these pages might have been the world she was supposed to seduce, her pose as good as a promise to deliver it to him. But when he tried to think about how someone else might react to such a ploy, he had to fall back on the wisdom of its purveyor.

He leaned back in his chair, out of the equation, only to find himself tipped suddenly into shadow. The reality of his office narrowed in on him, and, for a moment, in the dim outline of every little thing around him, his father's presence lurked, sober and proprietary—in the furniture, the work in piles and file cabinets, even the room itself, part of a decade-old division of a bigger space. It had been widely viewed as a magnanimous gesture on his father's part, this carving up of the magnificent head office to make room for his son, but Frank was wary of it, was always wary of his father's magnanimity. Now, for instance, he was being gracious—or what anyone else might see as gracious—about the transfer of power being imposed by the bank, and this was enough to make a person nervous, at least one who knew him well enough, as Frank began to suspect no one did. No one questioned his gracious resignation, any more than anyone questioned the premise for the change (except, of course, Melissa, who would challenge any portrayal of him as less than heroic). He was old, or older, certainly, but as canny as ever, and in the way he always was—covertly, circumspectly. In fact, there was no reason to believe that every quirk or lapse held up as evidence of his diminished powers was not simply another covert operation along a new route finally opened up to him by age. It made no obvious sense, but neither had his romantic raid on Annie, which would have seemed unthinkable until it happened, when the fact that it could be done became reason enough, or so his father's explanation went, to the extent that it went at all.

The women gazing up at him had assumed a mocking air, and Frank pushed them to one side. Just as he'd sought proof of his marketing plan in pictures he already knew, now he spread his desk with sheets of figures he could reproduce from memory down to the last decimal point and consulted these for evidence of the soundness of his projections and found some comfort in the circularity of the undertaking, his projections producing numbers that confirmed his projections. The plan had grown since he'd begun, shifting quickly from a conservative proposal for capitalizing stock to a radical one for complete financial restructuring, moving inevitably toward the sort of all-or-nothing approach that had always been anathema to Gutenbier in the staid, upright, utterly cautious form of his father. He had almost no doubts about his own ability, but he had a greater faith in his father's, which had all of Gutenbier behind it. He had an idea of vowing to pay should anything go wrong. The how of such an avowal was vague: though he did have a better sense of business than his sister, his notion of money, never having been an issue, was no closer than hers to the thing itself.

He extracted *Playboy* from the papers on his desk and started thumbing through it, gazing briefly at each girl with the benevolent feeling that she was trying to serve him. He was tossing it aside when his telephone rang, and Curtis Niemand said to him, "Frank, I have bad news. Your father's had a stroke."

When Curtis said his father was sleeping and couldn't see any visitors until morning, the chaos drained from Frank's throat and his chest and his stomach as suddenly as it had erupted, and he told the lawyer, as calmly as he could, that he would be right there.

6

Word of the old man's collapse sped around the plant. Alice had only the vaguest sense of moving in its wake. Mr. Johnson was a favorite among his employees—not so much because they knew him as because, depending on him as they did, they tended to confer on him whatever character their sense of well-being required—so that any blow to him shook them too. For Alice, though, the stir in the air was as new as everything else. She'd come into the worker's lounge feeling new herself, her crisp uniform laid over her arm, pressed against the perfectly white pair of sneakers wedged in the crook of her elbow. Her first thermos, shiny green, was nestled in the slotted lid of a matching lunch box that she carried stiff-armed, like a prop. In the locker room, which doubled as a lounge, painted wooden benches were pulled up around a central table, and on one of these two men were sitting side by side, tying the laces on their work boots, when Alice came in. One glanced up, nodded an acknowledgment, and stood, shaking his pants leg down over his boot, as the other gave his laces a last tug. When they moved, she found herself looking at a calendar hanging on the wall behind them, though as soon as she saw it she glanced away to scan the numbers on the lockers for her own, 17. A nearby door opened and closed with a clang, the smell of cigarette smoke filled the room, and the men left together, their voices echoing hellos down the hall, then sinking into the clamor beyond.

As she approached her locker, Alice slowed by the calendar, which was opened to January. The woman on the page was on her hands and knees, her rear rounded out. Stenciled on it, split by the strap of a G-string: PRIME CUT. She was gazing over her shoulder with a sleepy smile. It was the strap that Alice felt, creasing the same tender spot, and she stood transfixed and looked until she found herself in the woman's place, woken to Alex's prodding fingers, his knees pushing hers until she lay like a frog on her belly, stuck before she had the time to will herself away. It was maddening, especially after the secret stab of pleasure at the start, the way it always was—first the thrill and then the sorry thing itself—and by the time she realized someone else was in the room she'd come to think even the memory was a trick of the picture she'd been staring at. The master brewer, an old man named Martin, had paused at a locker a few feet from her. When she turned, he raised his eyebrows as if at a prank beyond them both; but she only lowered her eyes and shrank past him, heading toward the restroom to change.

There was one other woman in the lounge that morning, and Alice tried to catch her eye, but the woman only gave her a tired smile and kept unloading gear from her locker.

Just as her thoughts in their unwarranted way had fixed on the calendar girl, now they fastened on the other woman's smile; next thing, she was testing it, smiling wearily up at the blank row of lockers as she sat and bent to put her sneakers on. In the weariness, she felt a certain satisfaction that she thought the job would give her once she got used to it. She was training to be a technical brewer, which meant that she would someday be able to work in both the brewery and the bottling plant. These operations were separately housed, Little had explained to her, because of an old law that had something to do with taxes; the beer was piped under the road between. She was just lucky, he said, because things were getting so computerized that, even with the expansion after the fire, there probably wouldn't be very many more jobs. For now, though, Alice was supposed to master three or four tasks in the brewery and rotate among them, as all the other workers had done until they'd been at Gutenbier for a few years and new people like her came along to perform the simpler jobs. This, Little had told her, was how things had worked for him when, a year ago, he'd been bumped up to a broader category. And look, he was still low man among many who'd been there for fifteen or twenty years. That was why there were only a few women at Gutenbier, he figured, and those all hired since he'd started, probably an Equal Opportunity thing, though he also thought that women hadn't really started wanting to work here until around his time; that, and having Mr. Johnson's daughter up in the front office couldn't hurt.

Looking around her now, Alice saw only men. This was just what had appealed to her about the brewery, the air of industry men generated, the hum of them under the din of the machines as they went about their work, the purposeful scene so precisely unlike her idle and drifting days with Alex that it seemed to sum up everything she'd been missing—real life, she imagined it was. For minutes at a time she had the feeling she was pretending, that any second Alex might appear and tell her it was time to go home, at which she would rise up and float away, and nobody would notice, because she'd never really been there.

Presently she emerged from just such a moment to find that she wasn't doing anything. Sensing the patience in the pause of the man at her side, she lifted the keg that she was supposed to put on the racker. The machine conveyed the keg to a spot where it was hooked up to the filler and injected with beer at one end and carbon dioxide at the other, the pressure a careful balance, as Alice was instructed to observe. At the end, another man hammered in the bung with one swift and timely swing. Then he handed the mallet to Alice and stood aside.

As she was turning to the filler, she glimpsed Little, arrested in his work stacking kegs, watching her as if she might do something wrong. She threw her weight into her swing— just as beer geysered out of the bunghole and drenched her where she stood, her raised arm dripping foam. Moving with invisible speed, the man at her side plugged the keg. He was laughing. Alice realized the others were too. Everyone within eyesight had stopped, like Little, to enjoy her embarrassment.

Little was walking toward her, his lips in a line that quirked at the end like a grudging concession; otherwise his face was as blank as it had been a minute before. A hand came down on her shoulder, she started, and a jocular voice pronounced, "Consider yourself baptized," as the man who'd been teaching her said, in a tone in which humor gave way to matter-of-factness, "you've got between three and four seconds to get it. Nobody misses it a second time."

By then Little had reached her. "I've got a clean shirt if you want it," he said and started for the stairs. She fell in step behind him. For a minute he was silent. "It's a tradition," he said finally. "I thought about warning you, but"—he paused to look over his shoulder and shrugged—"you don't want to look like a sissy."

Alice was only half listening. She smiled, struck with the idea of an induction, herself as part of a tradition, the familiar figure "good sport." At the door the kneeling girl greeted her, smiling too, and for one stinging second Alice felt ridiculous. "Little," she said as she sat on a bench and looked straight up at the calendar, "what do you think of . . . ," and she nodded.

At his locker, he looked over his shoulder, then away, again with that beleaguered smile bulldozing one cheek, and busied himself with unwinding his shirt from around a pair of sneakers. Alice waited, and after a few more seconds, he shrugged.

"I don't like it," she said.

He said, "Take it down."

"I don't want it."

Little laughed. "You don't have to keep it. Just throw it away."

"You do it."

"It's not bothering me."

"But you won't look at it."

"OK," he admitted. "It might bother me to look at it if you're sitting here."

In the restroom, as she buttoned herself into his big shirt, Alice found a kind of comfort in it, and in his uneasiness, and his unwilling, almost woebegone smile, touching because of his size, an awkward fit. She remembered how he'd been as a boy, with all his lewd teasing and taunts when he hadn't known the first thing about sex except what he felt and that he couldn't do a thing about it. It occurred to her now, as it never had then, that he was a nice boy, and for an instant she felt a twinge of her old power to torment him just by being female, and with her new sense of his good nature, the feeling, once so dim and edgy, acquired a certain promising sweetness.

When she came out, he was gone, and the wall where the calendar had been was bare. She peered into the garbage can in the corner, and there it was, the grid of January lying flat, the woman crawling up the side. Alice frowned down at her for a minute. Straightening briskly, as if she'd never paused, she dipped her hand into the can and flicked the standing pages, which closed with a rustle as she walked away.

Even lying asleep in a hospital bed, in a tangle of tubes and wires, he was at the center of things, his heart making the whole room hum. If she kept her eyes on him, and her thoughts, willing him well, Melissa could stay safely within this web. It was a gift, given back after Sue's, where she'd found him on the floor, half buttoned in his twisted clothes, his silver hair sticking out like straw, his head lolled back while her friend tried to tuck his shirt into his pants, and he was speaking gibberish. Curtis had hunkered down at once and unbuttoned the buttons Sue had just finished fastening. She whispered at him, "He didn't have a *heart* attack," then edged a quick look at Melissa, and then the paramedics were there, clearing everyone away. As they rose with the stretcher, one said to Sue, seeming to know her, "I guess you got your story." She worked as a reporter for the local paper. Melissa stared at her, but she was already calling after the departing paramedic: "Don't let this get around or I'll be finished as an interviewer."

Now Melissa glanced down and found her father's eyes wide open, watching her. He asked her, "Do you love your brother?" His tone was only curious, as if this were the natural next question in a chat his importunate stroke had interrupted.

She was staring at him, examining the question as a trick symptom, the moment still surreal for her, when, with a therapeutic note of patience in his voice, he proposed an alternative: "Do you trust him?"

"*Dad.*" All her bated relief rushed into the word and she leaned to hug him, stopped, didn't know if it was safe, tried to fit the feeling into a squeeze of his hand. He was still waiting, though he smiled at her outburst as at a distraction. Frank? she said. Of course, she said, as if it went so much without saying that she'd overlooked it, not delayed, as his waiting made it seem. It wasn't an easy question—why else ask?—and why ask now?—and Frank was so ambiguous anyway. But, then, in some ways he wasn't. If, for instance, he had been the one, had been asked, Do you love your sister?, Frank would have answered without hesitation, because he would've known immediately what was wanted.

Her father could have been thinking exactly that. Or thinking nothing at all—he was studying her face in such a deliberate way, his customary way, that for an instant she had to remind herself he'd had a stroke and hadn't staged this scene. What he said at last was, "That's a comfort to me," his grave voice sinking so low that she had to bend to hear him, and even that close couldn't tell what reassured him, what she'd said or how, or how he'd heard it, the truth or the lie of it.

She'd been back at work no more than a minute before Frank appeared at her office door and asked, how was he? and then, hearing he'd been awake, what had he said? She said, "He asked about you."

Frank said, "I have a phone."

" 'I have a phone'? What does that mean? You have a phone?" she said. "You have a car. Frank, he had a stroke. He isn't going to call you up."

Frank was studying her as if he didn't find her quite convincing, any more than he believed the stroke itself, and for an instant she imagined he knew something, how they'd found him, what the banker had told her, what their father had asked, somehow saw it in her face, which must look guilty enough now to merit the scrutiny. But all he came up with was a sorry smile, a concession of sorts. "I know," he said. "I'm going back, tonight, right after work. Right now I'm sure he'd rather have me here."

She said, "I'm sure you're right."

"Did he say that?"

No, she told him, he hadn't said anything about business.

At this Frank nodded knowingly, even approvingly, his smug look as innocent as any of Jesse's, and it felt the same, closing on her heart. She knew enough never to be sure about their father, and for her there was a comfort like faith in the uncertainty, shaken for a moment maybe, but steadied again by his questions yesterday, which told her his mind was still working in its mysterious way. He hadn't said anything else. Evidently satisfied, he'd closed his eyes, and not a word she'd said had stirred him, and now the nurse said he had been asleep since then.

Melissa leaned a little closer, searching his face for the least hint of an expression. "Just don't die," she whispered at him, a subliminal charge—and suddenly his eyes were staring into hers. "Dad?" she started, but already they were closed, and when she'd found her voice again that didn't rouse him either. finally, she settled back into her seat, feeling the strangeness of that one startling look—like a glimpse of somebody observing her from behind her father's face, a brief, cold exposure.

She reached for the telephone on the bedside stand and dialed Curtis Niemand's number. Just as his secretary was telling her that he had already left the office, the door to the room opened, and there he was. She said, "I just called you."

"*Voilà.*"

"I was going to tell you not to bring Jesse, but . . ." Her hand made a magician's pass at the empty space around him.

"I thought I'd better check in first."

Together they turned to her father. "He's been out since I got here. Actually, since last time I was here, yesterday."

"But yesterday—?"

"He talked to me. He—Do you think he can hear us?" Glancing around, she found Curtis considering her as her father had the day before, with the same speculative interest. "Is my father up to something?"

"Melissa, he's unconscious." As if a look couldn't convey all he meant, he took her face between his hands, framed it for one gingerly instant, claiming her complete attention. "You mustn't overestimate your father," he said. It was something he'd done when she was younger, and now she felt herself fourteen again, warm as she was to the teasing of this man, in his early thirties then, when he'd stopped in precisely this way, in his sudden discomfort a thrilling acknowledgment. That had been the last time, though, and he'd withdrawn into an awkward formality around her, which the almost twenty years since had softened and refashioned into his present courtly manner. Then Curtis's gaze shifted, and behind her Sue murmured, "Melissa?"

As Melissa turned to see her, Sue looked past her at the bed. "How is he?"

"For the record?"

Curtis said, "I think I'll be going. Unless"—he paused as he passed Sue—"you'd like to have a lawyer present."

"Always."

When Curtis had gone Melissa told her, "He woke up and talked a little yesterday, but mostly he's out, and they don't know."

"Melissa, listen, I was just doing this Johnson thing, you know, the perennial Johnson thing about your glorious family. And I ran into your dad down at the Coop with Frank's fiancée. Annie Lowell."

"You don't have to tell me."

"*He* wanted to explain. Which is why he *called* on me, as he put it, to clear the air or whatever, and then we went to dinner, and thc rest"—she shrugged in slow motion, miming ellipsis—"you probably can guess."

"If I'm guessing correctly, I'd rather not." Melissa sank into the chair where she'd been sitting earlier. "You're both grown-ups."

"Yeah, free agents."

"Even though one of you is twice as grown-up as the other."

"You know, Melissa, there's just so grown-up a person gets, the way I see it."

"He's old enough to be your father."

"Except he's not. He's yours."

They stared at one another for a second, until Melissa burst out, would've wailed if she weren't trying to whisper, "Sue, it's so, it's just so—"

Sue said, "Actually—"

"I don't even want to know."

"Actually, I was about to say I'm sorry. Even though I told myself I wouldn't. But I am. It's not exactly what I expected either."

They sat in silence now, at least not staring anymore. Then Melissa said, "What was he doing with Annie?"

"Showing her a better time than Frank ever could?"

"You ought to know."

"Know what? Know which?"

"Either. Both. I meant my brother, how he wasn't quite a prince. To you, I mean. Because he can be. But that's all I meant: you have every right to say whatever."

"That's mighty liberal of you, Mel," Sue was saying, "mighty white," when a piercing buzz erupted from the machine next to her, an alarm sounded down the hall, and she began to chant as if the noise had sent her into shock, "Oh God, not while I'm here."

8

Alice had been at Gutenbier almost a week when the calendar reappeared. It was hanging just where it had been before, opened this time to February, with a cartoon balloon sketched next to the model's mouth, which said: LEAVE ME ALONE! Alice took this in with a glance as she walked by, not wanting to stop and look with the room full as it was. Anyway, the calendar didn't cast quite the spell it had before.

Just then her supervisor, Henry Graves, had stopped at her locker to tell her that this morning someone would be walking her through the brewing process, introducing her to the machines she would learn to run next week. Because Little had chosen that moment to pause in passing and say hello, Graves had given him the job of taking her around.

Now the filler sputtered out the last few drops of the brew, the meter registered two hundred barrels, and the men on either side of her moved to get the hose and pails needed for cleaning the machine. "That's it?" she said, not knowing if she should go yet.

One of them, a short and burly man called Cole, said over his shoulder in a tone of invitation, "You think you can squeeze any more out of it." A soft chuffing sound that might have been a laugh came from the other man, Hauser.

Going to her locker to get a sweater, since her circuit with Little would take her through chilly rooms, she found the lounge empty. Sweater in hand, she loitered a minute or so, then finally took a good look at the calendar girl, who'd been staring at her back all this time. The come-on smile the woman was wearing was so familiar that Alice didn't know anymore where she'd first learned it, but she'd worn it herself back when she'd still wanted to fascinate Alex and thought that required an effort on her part. And now the look gave her the strange little thrill that wearing it had once given her, and, feeling perfectly nervy, she stepped across the room and plucked the calendar off the wall. Then, for a second, she didn't know what to do with it, because the wastebasket had proved untrustworthy. Just as she was turning to put it in her locker, she realized she wasn't alone in the lounge anymore. Her supervisor was standing in the doorway, looking at her in a curious, calculating way. He smiled, and she relaxed a little.

"You wouldn't want to improperly dispose of company property," he said. He held out his hand, and she gave him the calendar, gladly. With an abruptness that startled her, he slapped the calendar against his thigh and told her, "I'll take care of this, don't you worry," and started out, only to come right back, shaking his heavy head and saying, "Damned if I didn't forget what I was doing." He took a folded sheet of paper out of his back pocket and waved it like a piece of evidence, pronouncing, "Softball." Little showed up to collect her just then, and they left Graves taping the schedule to the wall where the calendar had been.

The tour started in the upstairs room where the grain was stored, corn and barley in bins, roasted malt for their bock beer in bags. A brew was two hundred barrels, Little told Alice, and it took about a bushel of grain per barrel. He showed her how the grain was measured out with a bucket elevator, conveyed to the mill, dropped into the scale hopper, where it was weighed, then sent through a chute to the mash kettle on the floor below, all of this done with buttons and levers, much of it computerized and easily managed by one person. The first brew was started at five in the morning, he told her as he led her downstairs, and this part was called "mashing in," which meant cooking the grain or malt in water until the starch turned to sugar. Standing on the catwalk next to the enormous mash kettle, he pointed out the pipes for running in water and, above them, the lauter tun, where the brew was pumped next, for sparging, or straining the grits through hot water. The leftover grain, which they sold to local farmers, went into a holding tank; the liquid, now called "wort," was pumped back into the kettle, where the hops were added and the brew boiled for anywhere from an hour to an hour and a half.

Here Little paused to glance at her, and she gave him a nod that was supposed to convey her mastery of the material but must have fallen short, because he laughed out loud. "The first time you have to do this, someone'll be walking you through it," he said. "And that won't be for a long time. Never, if Graves had his way."

He wouldn't explain that, except to shrug uncomfortably and say that the supervisor was "kind of weird about women." Alice told him about her exchange with Graves over the calendar, but instead of drawing out Little, this only made him grimace, which he wouldn't explain either—leaving her to wonder why he'd brought up Graves anyway, and in such a tacked-on fashion.

All that was left, at least for this morning, were the cooling and fermenting phases. They'd already added the hops, he reminded her, and the brew had been boiling for, say, ninety minutes. So now it was pumped back upstairs to the wort chiller, the room he'd pointed out before they came down—she remembered, right? The wort had to cool to pitching temperature, or the temperature at which the yeast could be added, and that took about a minute for every two barrels, ninety minutes for a full brew. He showed her how the yeast was pumped into the beer line as the wort was run into a tank in the fermenting cellar. Every time the beer was moved now, he told her, it had to be tasted, the sugar and CO_2 tested, and the temperature checked, in case more yeast had to be pitched, but that was the brewmaster's concern. *Their* concern, he said, meaning his own and Alice's, was that it was lunchtime.

He turned and started off, going so fast that it took Alice almost two steps to each of his to keep up with him. She was still behind him when they got to the lounge. As she came through the doorway Graves caught her eye from the far corner of the room and, raising his arms like a coach, bellowed around, "Listen up!" The calendar was rolled up in one of his hands. Alice scanned the room. There were about thirty people in it just now, none of them paying much attention to the supervisor, who repeated his call even louder until there was almost quiet. "What I want to *talk* to you about," he intoned in his sonorous way, "is in*ter*ior design. This" —he unrolled the calendar with a snap— "is *some*one's idea of decor," and that made them laugh. "Can *any*one tell me what's *wrong* with this picture?" Lowering his head, he gazed out inquiringly from under his brow.

"Nothing!" the man called Cole volunteered.

Graves stared at him until the laughter died down. "Can *any*one tell Cole what's wrong with his bonehead answer? That's *right*, it's *bone*head. This" —he swept the air with the calendar, taking in the whole room— "is *not* a locker room."

Cole countered, "Yes it is."

"And *this*," Graves continued, "is not *every*body's idea of decor. I guess it didn't oc*cur* to our little design fairy that this might not be what Ms. Saxonberg wants to see when she walks in the door. Am I right, Alice?" Stricken, she glanced at him, then back into her locker, where for several minutes now she'd been fiddling with her lunch box, trying to look attentive and indifferent at once. On top of pointing her out, he'd used her married name—to show that he knew all about her, she thought. "From now on, I don't want you louts forgetting that we have a *la*dy in our midst. And anyone who offends Alice's delicate sensibility offends me. Boys?" He offered the calendar around in a sweep, but everyone ignored it, and little by little the room returned to its humming disorder. On his way out, without word or expression, Graves handed the calendar to the man whose locker was next to the door, the tall sullen one named Hauser who'd been on the racker with her, who just as blankly put it away.

When Alice found the nerve to leave the cover of her locker, one of the two other women in the room—the older, weary engineer named Mary—was walking past her and rolled her eyes in sympathy. The other woman, another apprentice brewer close to Alice's age, spoke up across the room:

"What if we put up pictures of guys, studly guys with tight little buns and—" A few men near her had stopped to listen; fixed in their attention, she concluded with a limp flip of her hand, "—whatever."

Mary, who'd been regarding her, asked mildly, "You think anybody would care?" The other woman considered this, and it wasn't until she and Mary glanced at Alice that Alice realized she'd been watching them, waiting for an answer—not so much to the question as to her own wonder about the exchange, which was like a foreign movie with subtitles, so much she must be missing because she didn't know the language.

That feeling of not quite knowing how people could act that way, as if nothing were personal when really it all was, followed her through the afternoon and imbued everything with a tricky significance, because as much as she thought she saw meaning in a thing, she suspected she was seeing things where there wasn't any meaning. For instance, when Chuck, who was showing her how to wash the aging tanks, told her to crawl through the manway ahead of him, she didn't know why he didn't go first, to demonstrate. She didn't want to be on her hands and knees in front of him in a hole, and then she was sorry she'd hesitated: if he hadn't thought twice about it before, now he might. Then, when they were inside, scrubbing the walls, and he sprayed her with the hose, it *seemed* like an accident, and he was very apologetic, but she just couldn't see how someone who'd been doing this for so long could be so inept. Her uneasiness didn't diminish until he left her to work on her own, and even then, alone inside a tank, she still somehow felt exposed.

While she finished the job, she had plenty of time to tell herself that she was just being silly. But the more she told herself, the more she wondered why she had to, if it was really so silly.

9

It was with something like envy that Curtis Niemand regarded Melissa and Frank. As the children, they were entitled to the consolation of extravagant grief, whereas he, as mere long-standing lawyer and friend, was expected to mourn but only so much and meanwhile had to go about his work, which in this case entailed making funeral arrangements for the man who'd been the mentor of his youth. Suddenly now he felt old—prematurely, perhaps, but truly old. It had come over him just as the doctors and nurses working over Francis had fallen still, as if he'd taken more than his share of life with him.

After first approaching Sue, who'd hastily corrected him, one of the doctors had given a somber but businesslike account to Melissa, and through it all she'd listened earnestly, nodding now and then, like an entrant in some solemn contest receiving her instructions. She picked up the bedside telephone, called her brother, and said, "Frank?" In a minute she was still frowning at the receiver in her hand, as if the phone and not her voice had failed her. Then she'd looked up and cast a puzzled glance around the room. When it snagged on him, the pain filled her face like a startled child's and she started to cry. The transformation was so abrupt and complete that it struck him with the full force of Francis's death, and he stared for what seemed like a long time before taking the few steps between them and putting his arm around her. With a hand to her eyes, she pressed her forehead into his shoulder and cried, her other hand opening and closing on his back, grasping without getting any purchase. He found himself holding her a little tighter, moved by her clasping hold on him, until, for no reason, something changed, and looking down at her, the clean part in her smooth black hair inches from his eyes, he began to feel anonymous. Melissa's sobs seemed to resonate through him, amplifying the emptiness and transforming it into longing, but as soon as he was conscious of the feeling, the voluptuousness of the moment passed. All that was left was the missing, tinged now with uneasiness, so that, when Melissa let go and stood away, frowning around absently as if he weren't really there, it was like a judgment rendered against him.

There was some penance in planning the funeral. With everyone else as good as immobilized, Melissa and Frank lacking the heart or whatever it took to tend to the necessary business, his practical activity had the peculiar consequence of making him the center of attention and authority among the mourners. That, he assumed, was why Frank kept turning to him throughout the funeral, then the wake. The wake, however, was a long one, with half of Rensselaer doing observance, and after a while the young man's hovering presence became disconcerting. Every time Curtis moved, there he was, close as an attendant. The effect was strangely conspiratorial, Machiavellian, Curtis would have thought had their roles been reversed, and this discomfited him even more, since it brought to mind how Francis had been about his son. It hardly seemed the time, paying last respects, to consider his friend's failure, whether as a father or as a judge of character. Once he'd thought of it, though, Curtis found it hard to think of anything else, and finally he felt compelled to take Frank aside and say to him, "I want you to know, Frank, I didn't write up your father's will."

Frank registered neither surprise nor offense, Curtis noted unhappily, and explained, "It wasn't something I felt I could do in good conscience. As a lawyer for Gutenbier," he added.

"In case of any conflict." A look of comprehension came into Frank's face. What he'd understood Curtis couldn't imagine, unless he'd mistaken "conflict" to mean that his father had left some of his stock in the company to his friend.

Meanwhile, Curtis made his way over to Melissa and Jesse. Melissa smiled when she spotted him, a quickening of pleasure so unconscious that when she caught herself she grimaced and sneaked a guilty glance around. It almost made him laugh. Then he looked up and found Frank watching them across the room.

What was it about him? Every advantageous feature of family, appearance, and character combined in him to create a subtle, unsettling effect—like one of those paintings that, though perfect at a glance, on closer inspection revealed all the strange distortions used to convey perspective. Now he was approaching, his hands half extended like a host's, his bearing somewhere between paterfamilias and heir presumptive. He stopped as his sister turned to someone else, and Curtis said, "I did witness it, though." A beneficiary couldn't sign a will, as Frank undoubtedly knew, so this would force him to rethink his interpretation of Curtis's qualms.

A red-haired young woman in the brewery blue was speaking to Melissa, standing close and looking up into her face with such intense sincerity that Curtis was surprised to learn from what she said that the two didn't know each other; the woman, a new employee, sorry that she'd never met Melissa's father, apparently simply had a gift for sympathy. This exchange seemed to have transfixed Frank, who couldn't hear a word of it from where he stood, Curtis was fairly certain. Then it occurred to him that Gutenbier was shut down for the day, so it might be the peculiarity of this girl's wearing her uniform anyway that piqued Frank's interest. When the girl broke off and eased away, with only a skittish look of recognition in Frank's direction, Melissa glanced at them and said, "Witness what?"

Frank's eyes were on him too, now that the redhead had

disappeared. "An accident," Curtis said offhandedly, and was pleased that the mayor approached just then to distract Melissa, if not Frank, who was studying him as if he were the problem. There was something oddly reassuring in the moment, a perverse satisfaction for Curtis when he thought to lean toward Melissa, away from Frank but not so far that he couldn't hear, and say, "Can I take you and Jesse home?"

IO

The beer Gutenbier made was heady and rich, darker than what most Americans wanted. It was also what most beer had been before innovations in bottling, refrigeration, and transportation made a product innocuous enough to please almost anyone both possible and necessary. Gutenbier, though well beyond icehouses and horse-drawn carriages, had not enjoyed the broader benefits of wide-scale technical advances in production and distribution—and so, when European imports and specialty beers came into vogue, it could enjoy the advantage of being small and backward. But, then, being small and backward imposed certain limits on the extent to which Gutenbier could enjoy its advantage. There were some people, Frank and the bankers among them, who thought the company should have gone much further, and when they looked for explanations, they focused first on the brewery's anachronistic regional habit, then on a phenomenon not unrelated to the first, its image. Gutenbier had made its name and money in the upper Midwest, chiefly in Wisconsin, among people who were mainly farmers and day laborers and hourly-wage earners. A picture of the lot of them would hardly sell Gutenbier to anyone who wasn't one of them—or even, Frank suspected, one who was. They were mostly the Midwestern poor or near-poor whose working and churchgoing and childrearing habits harked back to immigrant days, just as their drinking ways went to a time much further back and forgotten, when beer was a beverage of sustenance more than luxury, necessary as water and often safer to consume, and there was nothing particularly picturesque about necessity or convention.

If not for the experience of ending up in the same place with similar shortcomings, these people, from the Germans and Poles around Milwaukee to the Slavs and Nordic types of northern Wisconsin, would have insisted on their differences rather than their common traits, even now that the differences were more and more illusory. When they drank Gutenbier, in part because it was cheap, they were also capable of taking a certain pride in it because it was produced nearby. This translated into tradition, to which people ceased to give any thought, and they drank Gutenbier much as they drank beer, as a matter of course. Taken for granted even more than tradition was its cousin routine. An event like Francis Johnson's death reminded the townspeople that, as much as Gutenbier actually was to them, it also meant something more, though no one would want to have to say what. Chasing the late owner's wake with a beer, they found themselves wondering, almost to a man, what was happening in the world, what might explain the nostalgia for the passing moment and its spirit that seemed to be rising all around. That most of them didn't know Francis Johnson only made their loss all the more poignant, because it was bigger and vaguer than anything merely personal and all manner of possibilities and certainties attached themselves to it, so that this death, for one drunken evening, came to represent the end of an era of entrepreneurial verve, religious truth, and the family triumphant, whose waning explained a great deal.

What was odd about these beery mourners was the number of men in their twenties and thirties who were feeling lugubrious about the past that the late Francis Johnson represented at the moment. Little was among them, though not quite of them. Since he didn't have to go to work—the closing of the plant for the day was in itself enough to endear the departed

Mr. Johnson to all—he'd puttered around the house until the time came when, by the clock of his conscience, it was OK to start drinking; then he'd walked the six blocks to the bar he frequented, one of five within eyesight on St. Anne.

In reference to a new bar a few blocks down, which was called Jonah's Sports Bar and featured athletic diversions like a batting cage and a basketball hoop, this one had recently been renamed The Good Sports Bar and was referred to by its patrons as Losers. Inside, Losers was the sort of place that sunlight never touched, and it was just as well. What lighting there was took the form of advertising, as did the rest of the decor, the painted mirrors and posters above the bar and along the walls daubed with the dim colors of illuminated clocks and neon signs, all of them featuring the name of one beer or another. Among them, the Gutenbier calendar from 1970, opened to August, which was illustrated with a mountain vista faded almost to obscurity, looked more like a relic from ages ago than mere decades. Everything else, more recently provided by suppliers, was at least readable, and even the antique promotions—the saloon-type mirror touting Old Style, for instance—were more notable for their attempts to seem old than for their success in doing so. The posters that depicted young women in provocative clothing or poses could not have been more up-to-date, though the one by the table where Little sat down after picking up a beer at the crowded bar, a picture of a buxom blonde covering her privates and a bit of her breasts with the bottles she held, above the bold lettering HOMEGROWN IN MINNESTROHTA, had been rubbed clean at the crotch by a long succession of heads leaned against the wall when the bodies beneath them sagged. Little found the hole in the picture disturbing, though whether because it seemed prudish or sadistic or just plain seedy he couldn't really tell, so he automatically sat with his back to it. Spotting him from the end of the bar, Chuck crossed the room to take the seat Little hadn't.

Chuck was someone he'd known since high school, just well enough to know he didn't want to know him better. Older by a year, a football player, good-looking, and neither too smart nor too dumb, he'd been the sort of guy girls like Alice went with—and, in fact, Alice *had* gone out with Chuck. Since then, aside from thickening somewhat, he'd hardly changed. He'd managed to retain a sense of himself as someone people liked to be seen with, which, in a way, made his unwanted overtures easier to meet: understood as displays, they didn't require the kind of effort they never repaid.

"Who says money can't buy love," he said at last, raising his mug.

"You mean besides the Beatles?"

The two of them had lapsed into silence when Hauser hulked out of the shadow and claimed the other chair. "I never thought I'd be drinking to old man Johnson," he said, swallowing half his beer like a dose.

Finding himself flanked by these men, two of the very few of his co-workers he disliked, Little wondered what it was about him, what flaw in his nature, that attracted them, whether in fact it was the same one that kept him from moving now, a kind of inertia that somebody else might call easygoing. "What've you got against Johnson?" he asked, unconvinced, and Hauser conceded at once with a shrug.

Chuck said, "The old guy was all right. And I bet we're gonna miss him."

"Yeah," Hauser agreed. "Look what's coming." Chuck looked, and Little did too, and Hauser laughed. "I mean his kid, ya saps."

"Frank, you mean?"

"Yeah, Frank." Hauser, distrusting the obvious question, began to sound a bit annoyed.

"What about the other one, Melissa?"

"If you wanna start a day care. 'Human resources'? That was her brilliant idea. And those 'team meetings'?" He turned to Chuck, starting, "Isn't she the one," then noticed that not a word was registering, that Chuck was still staring at a couple of women he'd noticed when told to look.

"How ya doin', Chuckie?" Hauser said and poked him.

"Don't call me Chuckie."

"Still living in the pole barn?"

Chuck shook his head slowly, as if in dumb disbelief, and Hauser told him, "She'll come around."

In spite of himself, Little felt a twinge of sympathy for the guy. It was his experience that, once a woman evicted a man from his house, he wouldn't be moving back in, an observation he wasn't inclined to put forward. Instead, going on as if the last minute or so had escaped him, he said, "Frank'll computerize everything."

"Yeah," Hauser said, "my job."

"I don't know. If they're expanding like they say . . . What're you talking about anyway, Hauser? You know what they're like. I don't think they ever fired anyone."

"Yeah, but those were the old days."

"The old days? Like yesterday?" Hauser gave a grudging shrug, and Little admitted, "It'll be weird, though. My dad always talked about how it was when they went to the machines we have now."

He sank back, drifting into a daydream about times past in which his father's sunny dependability, that punctual smiling appearance each night, and his mother's kitchen and the pleasant hum and rumble of some horse-drawn Gutenbier of his imagination and the grace and ease of his first months of marriage or last months of courtship, whenever it was they were still holding hands, merged in one indistinct picture of everything he wanted. A sigh escaped him, and Rick, approaching, said, "Nice headrest, buddy."

Little sprang straight, so abruptly returned to the present that the usual drabness of the bar and its dim rendering of everybody there truly seemed the product of a precipitous fall. He got up, and Rick said, "Hey, buy me one, wouldja?"

The place seemed gloomier than anyone had seen it since

the Brewers lost the World Series in '82, as a man at the end of the bar was observing when Rick and Little approached. Sunny, the owner, who was tending bar, waved this away, saying, "You should've seen it the day Kennedy got shot."

Rick and Little looked at each other. "I was five," Rick said. "I was two."

Even the bad times weren't what they used to be.

With that, Little did finally reach a new low, while all around him the communal spirit that inhered in all he believed he was missing arose one more time, in the unlikely form of a wake for itself.

A mid so much epochal mourning, there was one point of pure grief. At eleven, Jesse hadn't lived long enough to suspect that the best was already past, or to learn that mourning might open the way to all manner of human sadness too deep and abstract for its own occasion. Simple and close and uncluttered by other losses, his sorrow consisted of missing his grandfather. He was at his computer, where he'd been ever since Curtis had brought them home, and, standing behind him, watching the screen ask him over and over what he wanted to do next, Melissa felt a momentary kinship with the machine.

"He was my only grandparent, you know," Jesse said without taking his eyes from the screen. This poor little bid for sympathy made him seem that much smaller, stranded, and she bent to wrap her arm around him, but he stood up, out of her embrace, and, announcing wearily that he was going to watch TV, headed for the basement.

The computer asked its plaintive question one more time. She reached to turn it off, but stopped, afraid she might wreck something. Feeling completely helpless, she looked down the hall where Jesse had disappeared. "I'm the mother," she explained to no one, sounding somewhat dubious, and the enormity of her loss, leaving her alone to be adult and wise when she wasn't, struck her with sickening force.

"You do fine," Curtis said, right behind her. His voice was so warm and familiar that for just an instant she was a child again herself, craving comfort. "It's something you never get used to," he said, as if to reassure her. "In all my years of being a father, I never once mustered the conviction to say, 'Because I said so,' and look at me now—I'm a grandfather too."

The thought, which for some reason, not just his age, seemed so unlikely, distracted her from her welling self-pity. Then he said, "I want to talk to you about your father's will. There'll be a reading for the board, but I wanted to prepare you."

"You mean about the stock."

"That, and other things. Your father named you his personal representative—what we used to call 'executor' or 'trustee.' An honor, maybe, but not what I'd call a favor." He proceeded to explain about seeing the estate through probate, how she would have to post bond to insure the sums she managed, substantial as these were, that she would want to retain an attorney—at which he tipped his hand and told her he could recommend a good one. She managed a smile and said, "I'll take that under advisement," and then he was sober again, frowning down a problem in the offing. He said, "How were you with the voting trust?"

"How was I what? You mean, what did I think?"

"In a manner of speaking. How did you see it working?"

"I guess I thought my father would keep running things, and we'd vote however he wanted. Assuming it happened. And the truth is, I never really thought it would."

"I think that's how he saw it too. In a way, that was how he saw his will, or at least he laid it out along those lines, with the minor drawback of his absence from the final picture."

"Minor," she repeated.

"Melissa," Curtis said, looking at some middle distance where the answer seemed to lie, "you know your father was forever rigging the world as a contest. And it strikes me that, in this case, you're going to have to decide for yourself whether what your father wanted was for you to have the running of the brewery or to have the say on Frank. And, of course, the rest of us."

"Well, what was it?"

"I honest to God don't know. But I can guess as well as you can that he didn't do it lightly."

"And do you think . . ."

"I think your father knew precisely what he was doing."

"Which was what?"

"I didn't say I knew."

"But you did. You do. You always knew."

"I know he was showing his absolute faith in your judgment."

"OK, look, I'm exercising my judgment and asking you, what would you do?"

He said, "Whatever you want."

They regarded one another then, the silence elliptical, until Curtis smiled, so unhappily and wearily that she felt her father's death all over again—but now, whereas it had been nothing but helplessness before, an absence and an aching, there was sympathy, as if Curtis's loss had moved in on her own, bringing a strange comfort with it. Even so she found she couldn't do a thing about it except look at him and, once he'd started for the door, watch him go.

By the time Alice went back out, it was late and her options had narrowed somewhat, since, of the taverns and churches that offered solace and inebriation of every sort to the lonely of Rensselaer, half were closed. Among the taverns, however, she still had plenty of choices. The smoky darkness of Losers repelled her, as did the noise of the sports bar. She kept walking down St. Anne until she came to the next bar, The Casino, a dim little place under the sign of two playing cards, and looked in. There were candles in netted red globes on the tables, giving off a warm ruby glow, and a few people sat at the bar, a couple of them talking without turning and the others absorbed in their drinks or the crooning of the jukebox. This was what she wanted by way of company, people talking a little but not necessarily to her, so she went in and sat at the bar.

Perhaps because of the feeling she got from her uniform, a sense of belonging but not here, strange and yet at home, she gave the impression of someone in costume, playing in a secret program known only to her but inviting speculation. It was not long before this air had its effect on a customer sitting two stools down, though all he could think of to say to her was, "Just get off work?" She told him no. He thought about that for a minute or so before trying again, this time to ask her, did she work at the brewery? Yes, she said, and, seeing his mistake, he tried a question that required more than a monosyllable in response. What did she do there? Everything, she told him.

Feeling lucky, the man drew closer. His move made her uncomfortable, and when she was uncomfortable she did what she'd learned to do around Alex, be attentive all around but make it look specific, put on a placating manner, in this case letting the man buy her a drink and not protesting when he got up as soon as she said she had to go, which seemed to him like the conclusion of an extended transaction and to her like one too, though of an entirely different sort. When she found herself outside with this drunk, friendly stranger saying, "Which way?" she simply stood there looking like a woman waiting for something to happen.

This was the scene Little came upon on his way home from Losers. He slowed to say hello, looking precisely like what she'd been expecting, a circumstance it took him a few perplexed seconds to appreciate. Alice was smiling, as she hadn't been until she'd seen him approaching, a subtle flattery he didn't resist. "Going home?" he said, after reviewing some of the possibilities the situation presented. Alice said, "Yes," and slipped her hand under his arm.

"Greg," Little said with a nod to the man, whose face and name he knew, though not much more, and walked on with Alice at his side. He understood enough not to make much of her hand on his arm, but was heartened somewhat when it stayed there. For the first few minutes, uncertain, he felt that Alice was in command, but as soon as he realized she wasn't letting go, he could start to see how he'd improved his position, maybe simply by not assuming too much.

They reached his house first, and he said, "Here we are." A minute of immobility passed before he asked, as a question, not an invitation, "Do you want to come in?"

His house was neat; it was a point of honor with him after his divorce. Pleased with its tidy appearance, he deposited Alice on the sofa and said, "Lct me get a few beers."

When he handed one to her, she said, "I wanted company," then explained, "I don't know anyone." When she added, "Everyone thinks I'm a whore," his disappointment was intense, because he knew what disabusing her on this count would mean, just when he was beginning to marvel at having a woman in his house again after ten o'clock, and one he'd wanted from the time he was thirteen. But of course he had to tell her, no, it wasn't so.

They sat like that for a few minutes, drinking their beers, Alice pensive, Little looking thoughtful, before he said, "Why are you wearing your uniform, Alice?"

"Because it makes me feel kind of invisible," she said. "I like it. I like working there. But that thing with the calendar, I don't know. Do you think I should play softball?"

"Sure. Lots of us do." In fact, now that he thought of it, an easygoing game seemed like just the thing. For a moment Alice filled his mind like a problem with many parts: how he wished she would fit in, because he didn't like friction, and how he also didn't want her to fit in, since he guessed that if she did she wouldn't turn to him anymore. She was looking at him now, or at least looking in his direction, her delicate face so close that all he was aware of was her body there beside him, shifting in such a way that he could almost feel the rough touch of the cloth of her uniform against her skin. It took a great effort to say, over the stirring of his senses, "Alice, don't you think you should go home? Or," he added, "you can stay here, I won't bother you."

"I am kind of tired," she admitted with a sigh.

He fetched her a shirt and a robe, a pillow and a blanket, and was retreating to his room when her voice, already soft and sleepy, rose from the sofa. "Little?" He stopped, not breathing. "You know what I'm thinking?" she murmured. "Maybe I'll get a cat." With a small, satisfied hmm and a rustle, she turned over, and he went to bed, resigned to a restless sleep.

13

There were a few hours each night when nobody was in the brewery. When the last person departed, Frank found that, engrossed as he was, he'd been waiting all the while for just this moment. The brick brewhouse was cool as a crypt and smelled as musty, and Frank took long deep drafts as he walked the old stone floor, stopping one night under the vast lauter tun, another on the stairs above the mash kettle, gazing around as if he found himself in an abandoned boyhood fort, where so much of his imaginative life was immured. If he could have he would have slept there, but for at least four and a half hours every night he did have to go home, and in this way a week had passed, leaving him not so much sleepy as restless on the Friday of the board meeting.

First he met with Randy Gold, who'd brought up some mock-ups, a reel, and a few of his colleagues from Dunwitty & Howard, all of whom, perhaps in concession to the backwater character of Rensselaer relative to their own Milwaukee, were sporting suspenders and neat short haircuts just shy of army issue and wearing the sleeves of their pastel shirts rolled up to the elbow. Frank worried about their credibility with the board, looking as they did like half the cast of a musical. Gold, more presentable in his business blue, began with disclaimers. As long as Frank demanded secrecy, he said, and as long as they hadn't been officially invited to pitch the account, there were certain limits to what they could do. Their excitement, however, was without bounds. They had taken his point, the sex angle, and incorporated the other sure thing—if there ever was such a thing in marketing—animal charm. The truth was, Gold averred, consumers responded better to animals than to people (except children, who were, sadly, out), and under cover of a creature one could get away with claims that otherwise might be laughed off the market. Could you assert, for instance, that a certain brand of scotch confers nobility? No, but you could say as much—and, what's more, say it convincingly—by wrapping the ad for the scotch around a lion. At this point, Frank began to grow impatient, always preferring a glimpse of the point over the story of how it was honed. Gold, perhaps reading this as skepticism, pressed on with greater vigor—finally arriving at the success story of Spuds Mackenzie, who had boosted the sales of Bud Light by 20 percent.

Frank said, "I never liked that dog."

While the young men lined up in their chairs looked on with quickened interest, Gold made a lip-show of starting to say something, thinking better of it, then going ahead: "But would you say you're the buyer you're after?"

"I drink beer," Frank said, but in a second had to concede that if a bull terrier whose charm was lost on him seduced so many buyers for Budweiser, then indeed he might not be the best judge of animal advertising. This brought about a palpable settling, and Gold, signaling one of his team to get the lights, slipped a videocassette into the machine.

Not nearly as rough as Gold had made them seem, the tentative commercials featured hikers, young men, stranded in a snowy mountain pass, until a St. Bernard came to the rescue, bearing a barrel of Gutenbier. Then, out of the storm, a troop of Alpine beauties appeared, their lederhosen cut as short and close as hot pants, their blouses, laced like corsets, spilling as much of their breasts as decency and the law allowed. The men reacted as if to a vision, only to be ignored by the women, who hunkered and cooed over the dog and helped themselves to his offering.

Then there was another, following a similar path to a party in a beer hall, the men finding that the hero's welcome they'd been enjoying was, again, meant for the St. Bernard who brought them in. Though not inclined to laugh, Frank remarked aloud that this was funny, even as he told himself that the great majority of buyers were vulgar—hence, the common man. "Right," Gold agreed, "that's what I call safe sex. All the bases covered. There's even the religious angle. It's a *Saint* Bernard. But the best thing is, this way you get a recognizable, lovable mascot that, along with the keg, has incredible merchandising potential."

"I'm more concerned about selling the beer," Frank said, "but that's fine."

Just then the intercom buzzed and all of them looked at their watches. When Frank answered, Joan announced Alice Reinhart.

"Does she have an appointment?" Frank was asking, as he tried to remember if he'd been apprised of Alice Reinhart's identity or mission, while the men began saying in a flurry of picking up and unplugging that they would go set up shop in the boardroom, when the young woman opened the door. Gold stepped to and held it open for her and subjected her to a disinterested appraisal as she stopped in the middle of the room and the other men trooped out, rolling the video equipment. "Why don't I come back in a few minutes," he said and slid out.

The girl was wearing a uniform from the plant. Though her name hadn't registered, he had seen her at the funeral and in fact had met her before that, on what had turned out to be her first day at Gutenbier. Now he was beginning to remember that she had some complaint, which was no surprise (since the workers never came to him for any other reason) but was surprisingly pleasant to contemplate all of a sudden. The girl had a certain pathetic appeal. It was, he supposed, something that occurred in the discrepancy between her native beauty and her rather trashy packaging of it, the gorgeous hair sprayed stiff as a wig, the makeup spread all over skin that otherwise was flawless, the greasy blue tracing the creases of her eye-lids—but then he caught himself making this critique and felt a flicker of irritation at Melissa, who had apparently become his template for women. As soon as he felt it, his annoyance showed up in the face before him as a wrinkle of anxiety. "Have a seat, Alice," he said. "What can I do for you?"

She glanced down at something in her hand, a wand of rolled paper, which she extended regretfully. "I found this on my locker."

He unrolled it, a poster, and read, under the boldface heading "Beer Is Better Than Women":

1. You can enjoy a beer all month long.
2. Beer stains wash out.
3. When your beer goes flat you toss it.
4. Beer labels come off without a fight.
5. A beer always goes down easy.
6. You can share a beer with your friends.
7. If you pour a beer right you'll always get good head.
8. A beer is always wet.
9. A frigid beer is a good beer.
10. After you've had a beer the bottle is still worth 10 cents.

After the first few lines, he kept his eyes scrolling while he wondered which was more distasteful, the thing itself or having it thrust upon him in this manner, and he reconsidered the girl. "Do you know who put it there?" he asked. "Or why?"

"Not really," she said, echoing his concern. "I took down a calendar someone put up, because it was"—she thought, her face a shifting picture of the effort, until she fixed on— "gross."

"Did you report this to Henry?"

"He saw me taking the calendar down, and he made an announcement about it, but the way he did it just made it worse."

"Ah," he said, "Henry," and leaned in confidentially, "is a cloudy thinker sometimes." He picked up the phone, dialed the plant, and had the supervisor paged. "I have Ms. Reinhart in my office," he said. "Henry, find out who put up that poster and suspend him without pay for a day."

This met with a brief silence. Finally Graves said, "Frank, you know I can't do that."

The intercom buzzed. "I know you can," Frank said, "and I know you will. Thanks, Henry." Alice Reinhart was watching his face with the intensity of a lip reader, but as soon as he hung up the phone she worked up a doubtful smile and, on second thought, stuck out her hand. Somewhat bemused, Frank shook it.

As she was leaving—from behind, in her bulky uniform, with her neck rising stemlike from the roomy collar, she looked like a child in a costume—he pressed the button on his phone, and Joan said, "Time."

14

Paneled in wood painted white so long ago that it had mellowed to cream, the Gutenbier boardroom, with its broad plank floor, oak table, and bank of enameled cabinets, bore a slight resemblance to the kitchens of old farmhouses found on the outskirts of Rensselaer. The atmosphere was generally homey too, though at the hottest peak of summer, through a flaw of ventilation, the building's fluky air conditioning seemed to pool its forces here. Coming in out of the heat and flushed with thinking she was late, Melissa felt the chill like the first clammy touch of illness. There was Frank, no doubt early, cool as ever, reading something in a folder as if he were quite alone—except that, just as she observed this, he looked straight up at her and smiled. Then someone she didn't know bent to say something to him and, following their glance, she noticed the video equipment set up at the far end, where her father used to sit, and with it, like courtiers stooping around a throne, three more strange young men.

"Frank?" she said. He lifted his hand from the table just enough to point, to what turned out to be an agenda lying right in front of her. The first item was "Francis Johnson's Will: Larry Hendler, Esq." That would be the colorless man sitting uneasily at one corner, his long hands folded over the briefcase balanced on his knees. Next to him, whispering without looking at each other, were Ernest and another Francis, two of her father's cousins, each of whom had a small share in the company; then Henry; Martin, the brewmaster; and Joan, Frank's secretary.

A few lines down she found "Advertising & Marketing, New Product." Though they'd been developing a new beer as they expanded the plant and equipment, this was the first she'd heard of its advancement to the realm of marketing, normally her bailiwick. It seemed somewhat presumptuous of Frank, unless it was something he'd worked up with her father, who probably would have told her. Thinking of the will again, what little Curtis had said, she felt her flaring annoyance fizzle in a rush of sympathy for her brother, who believed that an agenda put him out of uncertainty's way. Just then Curtis appeared at the door and she waved him over. As he was taking the seat next to her, she looked up and found Frank watching her, indifferent as before to everything else, including the stranger at his shoulder again, seeming so intent on deducing something from nothing she was aware of, her appearance, an expression, any unconsidered gesture, that she began to feel vaguely guilty about whatever it was. Curtis murmured something to her. He was still wearing a warm aura from the sultry day, and when it touched her like a blush, she looked from Frank to the agenda, fanned herself with it, and then felt Curtis watching her, apparently for a response. The lawyer Hendler cleared his throat.

Everyone went silent, although for a second it seemed her hearing had stopped and there was nothing but her heart pounding, a dull throbbing in her ears. There was no precedent in memory for a meeting without her father. The bankers' claims aside, he had controlled Gutenbier as president and chairman as much through natural authority— simple fatherhood, it had always seemed to her—as through the power conferred by his holdings, 70 percent of the company's active shares. He'd owned a full 90 percent until he'd pressed her into the service of Gutenbier, when, as an incentive, though Frank didn't need one and she didn't want one, he'd given each of them 10 percent of the stock.

"I won't take much of your time," the lawyer said, extracting one sheet of paper. "This," he remarked, sounding somewhat bemused, "is a peculiar document. Or, I should say, a document peculiar to Francis. 'In fine fettle,' it begins, 'I, Francis Albert Johnson, residing et cetera and assuming my inevitable death, bequeath my worldly goods as follows'—and I'll limit myself to the immediate business, which is to say, the business—'Of my one hundred and seventy-five thousand shares in the Gutenbier Corporation I leave eighty-five thousand to my son, Francis Albert Johnson, Jr.' " Melissa tried to smile at Frank, but he seemed not to see her. " 'And,' " the lawyer went on, " 'ninety thousand to my daughter, Melissa Margaret.' " The numbers were oddly calming. As Hendler explained that nothing else really concerned them, she calculated the bequests, a 2-percent difference between them, precisely the difference in years between her and Frank, then realized Frank was staring at her, fixedly, no doubt calculating too, and her first magnanimous feeling swept her.

With the stock they had already, this gave her a 46-percent share in the company, Frank 44 percent, neither the controlling interest. She could see how, with Curtis's 7 (the uncles shared 3 percent—inherited from her great-uncle, on whom his father, Melissa's grandfather, had taken great pity or perpetrated a great fraud, depending on which strain of the family was making the accounting), the three of them would run things just as Curtis had suggested, though she, the older, with the bigger holding, would be nominally in charge—it was all quite right, and suddenly her eyes were filling with tears. This surprised her just enough to put a stop to it. She looked to Frank for some sign, but he was looking at Curtis, sympathetically, it seemed, although that mystified her; she couldn't check Curtis's expression without being obvious. Then he started conferring with Hendler about how business was to be conducted during probate, the other lawyer passing around copies as he spoke. "Melissa?" Frank said. She was reading the will, her first glimpse: other than gifts to the staff and tokens to friends and distant family, everything was going in trust to Jesse—and whatever other "posthumous grandchildren" she and Frank saw fit to produce. "Melissa?" Frank said again, his tone modulating toward insistence, though his face when she looked up, slightly dazed, was an image of patience.

"Yes," she said, "well, maybe we should vote. I'm guessing things'll go on as they were, but with the breakdown in stock what it is, I probably should step in as chair, as a formality anyway. Unless anybody . . . ?"

Frank had his chin propped on his hand, his thumb and forefinger framing his mouth, his frowning eyes downcast in a semblance of hard thought, and when he raised them his brow furrowed once more with deliberation. "Maybe," he said, "because you have the edge in stock—and you'd have the voting advantage regardless—it might be wise, in terms of balance, if I took on the titular role."

This made Melissa laugh. " 'Titular role'?" she repeated, delighted. "Frank, it's not a majority, voting won't matter. . . . Anybody?" She glanced around the table. "Move to vote?"

Uncle Francis seconded, as was his habit.

"I guess I'm already on record," she said, "so let's go from here. Curtis?"

"I don't know that I care for how that motion was framed, but my seven says aye to Melissa."

It was then that she looked across the table at her brother and saw, in the instant before he woke to it, how he was staring at Curtis, his shock unmistakable, no expression at all, strange and suspended upon the lawyer, who wasn't even looking his way. She might have thought nothing of it if not for the way Frank, as soon as he saw her watching, tried to work his shock into an elastic grimace, an exercise, as if the face she'd seen were just the blank reflection of a momentary daydream. She shifted her gaze and found the uncles watching Frank as well, like a couple of troubled children, though when she looked their way they quickly said in unison, "Aye," to which Ernest added, for the sake of perfect clarity, "Same here, Melissa."

That brought them all back to Frank, who spread his hands

in ceremonial fashion and pronounced, with a broad smile, "So that makes it unanimous."

Doubting his smile, she produced one of her own with some difficulty. "And you'll be president, Frank," she said, and was sorry as soon as she heard how it sounded, the echo of playing office all those years ago, when she'd been just as nonchalant about being the boss. But then there had really been nothing to letting Frank have his way, whereas now she couldn't see how to get out of it without trouble. She would seem silly, as nonchalant as she was, a blow to the authority she had so blithely assumed and now found herself maintaining even at Frank's expense. It must mean something, more than she'd suspected, though that didn't make her feel any better about the whole business; worse, in fact, and she hurried the meeting along toward agenda item number four, "New Product," etc., so Frank could take the floor.

15

A rational man, Frank explained his situation to himself in a few ways, then settled on two: His sister was simply confused, because their father would never have been so doting as to entrust her with the future of the brewery and never would have dreamed that she would take it upon herself. More than once, when Melissa was still resisting Gutenbier, barely making it to a meeting a month, he'd actually told Frank that what she was doing was "more important," although Frank was hard put to say what precisely that was, besides being a mother. Back then her mothering impulse had seemed too much for one little boy to absorb, and she had worked off the excess at the local food shelf and at a halfway house. He couldn't imagine her there—the vacant-eyed men touching her arm and telling her about the things they'd done, what they regretted, what they wanted; the women seeing in his sister a soft touch, so accurate in their assessment that she'd even hired one after another to help her around the house, where one had helped herself to the stereo and television and another, the last, had smacked Jesse for making a mess. As much as there was to be said for such softness, this was not the kind of judgment his father could possibly have equated with leadership, leading as it often did to the sort of sentimental miscalculations that undermined the very structure on which generous principles like Melissa's so unwittingly rested. Her mistake was probably predictable.

But then there was Curtis, surely a different case. The second possibility presented itself as Frank considered the lawyer: There was no misunderstanding. He was being tried. This fit the way he felt so well that he lingered there a minute, trying to get a better look at it, his father's perpetual demand for proof finally formalized as a test—and only then, in the strange and roomy comfort of the moment, did he see how his world had narrowed on him, how small and dark and cramped it had become precisely when it seemed that every opportunity he'd been denied should be opening to him.

While Melissa went over the numbers—the sales and the orders and, with Martin interjecting, some anticipated problems procuring corn and hops from their suppliers in this hot, dry year—he began to change his plans for financing Gutenbier Light. Rather than borrowing against anticipated gains, he would suggest issuing more stock, and meanwhile he could figure ways to get around the rights issue, which, in view of his sister's constant cash-flow crisis and the bond she'd have to pay as executrix along with inheritance taxes, might not be too difficult. He could improve his position even further by proposing that dividends be issued in stock instead of cash. For the first time in what certainly was weeks and felt like longer, he started to feel right with the world again. Even the worst of it, this business of the *image*, seemed within his grasp, and when Melissa, none too unhappily, turned the meeting over to him, he quickly made the mandatory speech: whatever he could do to ease the company through this difficult transition. He then reminded them of the feasibility study conducted last season, and introduced Gold and his Dunwitty colleagues as the team who would be test-marketing the new beer. He raised his two fingers in the Christlike gesture he'd seen Gold make, and, magically, the lights went out.

Unlike his office, this room was without ambient light, so all he could see of the faces ranged around the table was the bluish glow of the commercials flickering across their features. The silence, broken only by the chuckles of the Dunwitty men, was no more expressive. When the lights came up he looked around, leaving Melissa till last, only to discover that she too was scanning reactions, and was just about to come back to him in her survey. She was wearing her thoughtful expression, a widening of the eyes that suggested room for whatever idea or opinion she might encounter. Curtis was inscrutable. The others seemed pleased. Gold, who had risen to stand by the monitor, said, "We'll be ready to air spots locally and in Kansas City in under three weeks."

"Kansas City?" his bewildered sister said. "Three weeks?"

"It's only a test," Frank told her. "We wouldn't be ready to go to mass production for months. And wouldn't want to, not until we see how this goes. And what kind of money we can drum up. Where do we stand on the beer, Martin?"

"Next week," Martin said.

"What?"

"Finished. The beer."

Frank tried to read his sister's expression. "I guess . . . ," she said and stalled, evidently overwhelmed by the variables. "I guess my first question is, is it legal?"

"Parody," Gold answered in the affirmative. "Covered."

"Wouldn't it be funny, I mean maybe just as effective, if they showed up wearing snowsuits or something, you know, bundled up to their eyes? I'm just wondering about our women customers."

"All fifteen of them?" Frank said and got a laugh. "No," he said, "forget our customers. They drink Gutenbier. We want the people who don't."

"But if it's a light beer . . ."

"You know that's the market. The superficially health-and-appearance-conscious man under thirty."

"Under thirty by a good ten years," Curtis observed, and Gold said brightly, as if from above, "The point is exposure. Carpet bombing. Show it and show it and show it."

Frank turned to Curtis. "You don't approve?"

"I have my doubts about the whole enterprise. Doubts about what the market will bear in terms of one more beer like so many already out there, while we risk messing up the market we've made over so many years for a beer that's unique."

"Curtis, Gutenbier isn't going anywhere."

"No?"

"No. This is strictly about the new beer."

"And I can't say I relish the idea of releasing this . . . carpet-bombing campaign on the heels of your father's death. It's as good as saying we were just waiting—"

"Curtis?" Melissa spoke softly but with an urgent undertone, which Frank understood as soon as he felt her checking his own expression. His sister was protecting his feelings, so raw after he was robbed of his rightful control of the company. Annoyed as he was, he undertook to look pained, and knew he'd succeeded when she lied outright: "My father was behind this from the first. Behind Frank," she added. "We're going to have to have a special meeting next week, so let's hold off on this. Frank, were you going to say something about the financing?"

He said the ads in their final form would be part of the prospectus given to interested parties once the company announced a stock offering in the financial press. That was one way of raising capital; however, if they wanted to protect their close holding of the company, they might find an investor to buy the stock with an option to sell it back at an anticipated profit—in effect, an approach similar to borrowing against their expected gains, but not so costly to the company. Furthermore, they'd conserve capital by issuing stock in lieu of dividends. He watched as the words slowly worked their sense on Melissa.

"Let's look for an outside investor," she said. "I'm assuming you have someone in mind. Frank, what's—if this doesn't fly, what's our risk? Worst-case scenario, where do we stand?"

He reviewed the encouraging research, reiterated their plans to test first, then start slowly, and finally said, "Worst case? We have a new substantial stockholder."

PART TWO

16

The Little Leaguers were still on the field when Little got there, so he sat and watched awhile. The pitcher, a lefty, was winding up to his windup. He pawed the mound with one foot, then the other, touched his cap and tapped his elbow, suddenly drew himself up short, glaring at the runner leading off first base. Little would've laughed but didn't, because, funny as it was, he remembered how it felt, even still felt sometimes. The pitch was wide. "OK, Jesse," the coach called, and the boy settled into his routine again. Little watched in surprise as the next ball broke to the left, catching the batter out.

Melissa Johnson was making her way to where the softball teams were assembling, her head turned to watch the field, and when she whooped, Little looked at the pitcher differently. The boy reacted to her yell with a quick, involuntary look that didn't quite find her. "Your kid?" Little said, when she reached him, and she grinned. "How old?"

"Eleven." She said it ruefully.

"Nice screwball."

She squinted at him with her head slightly atilt, her smile bated, and Little thought about explaining but decided against it, afraid he might offend her. He liked her—it was more than just not minding her—and he didn't know why, since he didn't know her, except to say hello. He noticed Alice wandering toward them. She was wearing her uniform.

"Are you playing?" he asked Melissa, trying for a tone that balanced camaraderie and respect.

"Yes," she said. "Not that I have since high school."

"That's all right. It's mellow. Anybody gets too serious," he thumbed like an ump, "they're out."

Her smile when he said this was warm in a way he was used to from women not so much put at ease as grateful for the attempt. Alice reached them just then, and he said, "Melissa Johnson, do you know Alice Reinhart?"

"We've met," Melissa said, shaking Alice's hand—and though she was nice about it, she somehow seemed like the boss again. Alice, for her part, was staring as if starstruck. It made him vaguely uncomfortable, as did her uniform, when everyone else would be wearing shorts or jeans, so he said, "Just come from work?"

She blinked. "What do you think?" she said, as if this were the only reason in the world that she'd be wearing these clothes. Then she smiled at Melissa, and he felt he'd entered strange new territory, a female place. Just then Chuck's appearance, something he'd never imagined he'd welcome, offered escape, and Little took it.

Henry tapped the keg and was assigning teams, telling Melissa Johnson first, in an avuncular fashion, "You just stick with me," when the woman's son came up, not quite to the crowd of adults, and stood there, dangling his glove, till he caught his mother's attention.

"Hey," she said, "nice screwball."

This earned her a look a lot like the one she'd given Little. Then the boy said, "I'm going with Paul and P.J., OK?"

"Where, to Paul's?"

"I guess."

"His mom's there?"

The boy nodded and shrugged at once, and his mother bent to put her arm around him, bringing such an exquisite mixture of love and embarrassment to his small face that Little felt it too.

"Mary's pitching!" Henry yelled to Hauser, who was setting

out the bags and now went back to adjust the pitcher's plate, only to be told by Mary to leave it where it was. "Get that keg out of the sun!" Henry yelled to no one in particular, then added in a booming voice, "And remember, ladies and germs, this is steroid-free softball!" He started herding his team into the dugout, while Steve put on his catcher's mask, Cole trotted out to second, Hauser to third, and the rest straggled onto the field. Mary beckoned Hauser over with her mitt, and some shuffling ensued, with Leah, who'd gone out to play left field, called in closer, Kenny sent out in her place.

Chuck led off, hit a line drive right past Hauser, and landed on first, grinning. He was already out of breath, but Little gave him a slap on the back, knowing how much athletic prowess, even if it was mythical, meant to the man. Rick was up next and grounded out, and Little started to relax into the rhythm of the game. When Alice's at-bat arrived, he suffered a momentary pang, seeing how stiff she was; but she just struck out, swinging, and nobody said anything one way or the other, and he was relieved to think that he'd been right, telling her to come and be one of the guys.

It wasn't till the second inning that Melissa Johnson came up to bat, and Little felt it as a subtle tension even before he noticed how everyone was watching, caught between wanting the boss to do well and hoping she wouldn't. She slugged a ball all the way to left field, surprising everyone, including Kenny, who watched it go, and apparently herself, since she just stood there until Henry bellowed at her, "Run, you . . . boss!" Then she took a lead off first, and Little, trying to be discreet, told her to come back. "Why?" she said. He told her it was softball rules, you couldn't leave the base until the ball left the pitcher's hand, and, looking highly skeptical, flush with her first hit, she said, "You know, I can have you fired if you're lying." This was so unexpected that when he laughed it came out like a cough. "You do and you'll never play softball again," he said.

By the fifth inning, everything seemed perfectly fine. The sun was starting to set, giving the sky a rosy glow that matched the feeling that had come over him after the exchange with Melissa Johnson and his own not-too-shabby performance and a few glasses of beer. Alice had even gotten on base, on a walk. When Melissa came up again and got to first with a grounder, he greeted her like an old friend. Hauser walked up to talk to Mary, and Kenny came in too, and Melissa, squinting at this colloquy, uttered a suspicious, "Hey, what's going on?"

Little said, "Conference on the mound."

She seemed to want to have one too, and he was trying to explain, without sounding patronizing, that this wouldn't be appropriate, when Hauser and Kenny spread out again and Mary raised her arm to pitch and Alice decided to steal third. Little winced.

Melissa said, "What?"

"She can't do that."

"Steal?"

"Same thing I told you before."

But Cole, of course, didn't bother to tell Alice anything. He just waited until Kenny lobbed the ball to Hauser, then started moving in. Caught, Alice turned to go back, and Hauser threw the ball to Cole. She turned again and made a start and stopped when Cole tossed the ball back to Hauser. Watching as she stood there weaving, her eyes darting between the men, Little tensed. A frown crossed Melissa Johnson's face. "Can they do that?"

"Well . . . ," he said, distracted, as Cole and Hauser closed in on Alice. She made a quick move as if to duck around Hauser; they both shot forward just as quickly and—it seemed like an accident—sandwiched her between them. Because it looked so comical, a trick of timing, everyone on the field burst out laughing, while the dugout erupted in a disgruntled lowing. Melissa Johnson, however, was uncertain. When she looked at him, Little said, "If people at the plant were bothering someone—I mean another employee—would you want to know?"

"Of course," she said, but then, short of ratting, he couldn't think of anything to say, especially in view of the dubious circumstances of the episode they'd just witnessed. Anyway, Alice seemed OK walking back across the field—a bit stiffly, but she'd been a bit stiff all day. Melissa Johnson was still looking at him, so close and concerned that it made him uncomfortable, like a reluctant good little boy. "*Would* I know?" she said—but a hit interrupted and she had to run.

Rick raced to first, folded to catch his breath, and cocked his head to say in mocking disgust, "You brown nose."

17

For his firm, Curtis was representing another local company, Winston Trussworks, against an injured employee who (or whose insurance company) was claiming that the company had been recklessly remiss in putting him in the way of a crane that had swung a beam into his back and broken his spine. Terrible as it was, it was what anyone outside a jury would have deemed an accident, but the grievous nature of the injury cried out for compensation, which in turn required that blame be assigned—and nobody but the Trussworks could afford that kind of reprobation. For the company it was necessarily a matter of economics, compelling him to press for a "reasonable" settlement, which meant whittling away at the "unreasonable" complaint of a paraplegic, a prospect that made Curtis long to be, just once, on a jury where he might blithely award all of someone else's money to some needy soul.

Lillian Roth, opposing counsel and presently opposing him across a tiny table at the Greenleaf Tavern, was free of such qualms. The fineness of her expression, all focused in the clear light of her eyes, was an advertisement for a certain virtue unsullied by practical constraints. Her hair—quite white, as it had been as far back as Curtis could remember—framed her delicate features with a sort of maternal authority, and her ability to nurse one glass of white wine through the duration of his two beers seemed somehow to bear out this impression.

They'd been getting nowhere for a good twenty minutes and had finally turned to local politics when Lillian was distracted by something on the television suspended in the corner. Curtis craned his neck to see, and what he saw was the commercial for Gutenbier Light that he'd seen at the board meeting, virtually unchanged. Surprised—they hadn't yet met again—he composed himself before turning back to Lillian. Her steady examination wore away at his nonchalance, and at last he raised his eyebrows and said with finality, "A test. Somewhat rough," he added.

She considered him for another long minute before saying, "Are we assuming women don't drink beer?"

"Present company excluded?" he said, and she paused in the middle of lifting her wineglass and gave it an abstracted look.

"Or, no, wait, I think I see," she said speculatively, as if speaking to herself, "it may be women i*den*tify with comely lasses like those, and they're sitting around awash in nostalgia for the days when the only restraint they had to worry about was a corset."

"Would those be the women who read *Cosmopolitan*?"

"Meaning?"

"What does that ad have that the cover of *Cosmopolitan* doesn't?"

"An audience who tuned in to see the evening news, for instance? Instead of one who bought the—"

"Lillian, it *is* an ad."

"Right, an *ad*, what was I thinking? Of course there's no relation between an *ad* and how the boys at Gutenbier do business."

"You know that Melissa's chair now?"

Her gaze kept after him, unmitigated. "Yes. I never figured her for the type."

"What type would that be?"

"Gets into the club, discovers that—*mirabile dictu*—she likes it, and pretty soon the privileges and power go right to her head and she's doing enforcer duty."

Briefly he was speechless, then managed a cautious protest. "The situation's somewhat more complex."

"No doubt."

"And, after all, this is fairly innocuous."

"Oh, fairly certainly."

He was choosing his next remark, looking for one demanding more than an echo, when he noticed Frank coming into the bar. Peering around as if shopping for facial expressions, he caught sight of them and cut toward their table. "See the spot?" he said, then nodded: "Lil." His nervous enthusiasm moved the air around him.

Curtis said, "We were just talking about it."

"It's what's called a teaser," Frank informed Lillian.

"Ah," she said, her facetiousness so patent, Curtis was amazed when Frank went on to explain.

"Advertising the product before it's available. Whet the appetite."

"How true," she said. "I find I'm ravenous." Frank meanwhile was acknowledging someone beyond them with a subtle upward movement of his chin. Now he excused himself, and Lillian's gaze followed in his agitated wake for a few curious seconds. When she returned to Curtis, they regarded one another with a shared bemusement.

"Wait and see?" he said, getting up after a pause.

"Right," she said, "a teaser."

His drive home took him past the park where the brewery team was playing ball, and, making out Melissa on the field, deep in conversation with the third-base coach, he stopped. Cool as the lavender twilight seemed from his air-conditioned car, the air when he emerged was still as sultry as it had been all that day, all that week. Watching, waving when he thought he'd caught Melissa's eye, he strolled over to the keg set up behind one of the dugouts. There he came up behind Jesse, who was waiting for Chuck to draw him a beer, the avidity of his interest apparent in his posture and in the quivering of the two brimming cupfuls he already held. When he turned around, right into Curtis, he stopped short and sloshed and then, after the barest dumbstruck instant, said in an attempt at offhandedness, "For my mom." Chuck smirked.

Beyond Jesse, Curtis could see two boys lurking at the far edge of the park. "Then why don't I hold them?" he said, reaching for the cups. "I have to talk to her anyway. Becoming quite the drinker, your mother," he remarked as he balanced the third cup between his fingertips and Jesse stole a regretful look at his lost prize.

The boy stood there uncertainly. "Actually, I could use one of these myself," Curtis said. "Chuck?" And he extended his full hands toward the man, who was taking the precarious cup when a commotion on the field caught their attention—the winning run, it seemed. From the fracas, a crush of slapping hands and shoulders, Melissa emerged grinning and made her way to him, her blue jeans dirty at the knees, her dark face flushed and long braid bouncing as she walked, so girlish it seemed unlikely she could be the mother of this boy—when Curtis glanced back, it was just in time to see Jesse join his friends in the dusky distance.

He was about to offer Melissa a ride when her friend Sue appeared and planted herself in front of Melissa. "When are you going to stop not talking to me?" she asked.

Melissa blinked like someone waking. "I'm not not talking to you."

"When's the last time you talked to me?"

"The last time I saw you."

Sue shook her head ruefully. "No," she said, "that was your father's funeral, and nary a word was exchanged—which was fine—but technically . . . "

Melissa frowned and flickered a look past her at Curtis. Immediately Sue turned to find him. "You again," she said.

"Who else would I be?"

"OK, Sue." Melissa's voice tugged her friend around. "Here I am."

Even from behind, Curtis could read the woman's exasper-

ation, in the precipitous slump, the backward roll of her head.
She said, "You know what I mean."

"Then call me."

"Why should I always have to be the one who calls?"

"You're the one who wants to talk."

"So you don't."

Lowering her brow, Melissa directed a level look at her
friend, who subsided almost at once, and Curtis started to suspect that what he'd witnessed was not a real exchange but a
ritual, evidently satisfactory to both women, since Sue fell in
step next to Melissa now and said in a new, casual tone, "So
what about this Gutenbier Light?"

"It's a new beer."

"Duh. It sure has Frank's grubby little paws all over it."

"Bitter, bitter."

"No I'm not."

"How'd you know about it?"

"The grubby little paws?" Sue emitted a mocking chortle.
"I have my sources," she said, "i.e., TV."

Curtis, who'd fallen in behind them, spoke up. "That's what
I was hoping to talk to you about. If you need a lift home—"
Under Sue's scrutiny he suddenly felt like a stranger beckoning to a schoolgirl from a black sedan. Then Melissa smiled
and said, "Sure," and the feeling evaporated.

The minute they reached his car, Sue assumed a wistful
look, like someone left, so Curtis made himself say, "Like a
ride?" Her eyes narrowed at him in that suspicious way she
had of focusing. "I have a car," she said. As he drove away he
could see her still standing on the curb, presiding over the vacant place.

"I was at the Greenleaf with Lillian Roth," he told Melissa,
"talking shop, when the ad came on." He turned to find her
waiting blankly. "The commercial for the new beer?"

"It did?" Then, smoothing her confusion into a semblance
of assurance, she said, "It's just Frank. It's his thing, and he's

trying to do it all, so he doesn't look— He has to make up for not being chair."

" 'Make up' is a somewhat loose interpretation."

"Well, it *isn't* fair. Is it? I'm— He's always trying so hard. He reminds me of Jesse sometimes, all that earnest concentration, so eager, and . . ." She fluttered her fingers, summoning the right word.

Curtis obliged: "And all grown-up. Let's say you're erring on the side of sisterly love and leave it at that. Meanwhile, I was about to say: Lillian's reaction would seem to confirm your doubts."

"About the ad? You don't even have to tell me. She's so . . ." With a sigh, Melissa intimated everything exasperating about Lillian Roth.

"And you're a traitor to your sex."

"She said that?"

"Words to that effect."

"We're stuck with the ad campaign. What am I going to do, fire Frank? I say we wait and see how everything goes."

"And if it doesn't?"

"I'm not saying we can't have a contingency plan."

Her eyes wandered to the window and, gazing out at the darkening town, she laid her head against the headrest; there it stayed for the remainder of the drive.

At her house she asked him to wait because she had to water her delphinium, which made no sense to him except that she was asking something of him when he was especially willing, and so he stood there until she reappeared with a flashlight and turned it on, having him hold it while she unwound the hose. He aimed the light up and swept the eaves, picking out two outdoor lamps. "Burned out," she said, without looking up, then explained that the plant in question had been given to her by one of her "clients" at the shelter. Curtis panned the border with the flashlight, revealing a ragged collection of flagging plants, here and there among them splashes of daisies that were either healthy or weeds.

With the evening no coolness had come down, and in the warm dark the world was like a room, closed in and full of the heat of the day and the smell of parched grass and earth and wilting flowers. Watching Melissa tend to the plant, he was aware of a certain pathos about her bent figure; for the first time he saw her solitary, without the crowd of intimates he imagined encircling everyone besides himself. What he had instead—his oldness, that withering in on himself that he'd felt under her girlish smile—seemed to loosen its hold. Then it fled altogether, leaving the two of them as the sole occupants of this warm room of the world, Melissa the delicate, bending one. When she straightened, he put his arm around her. She turned, looking startled, but as soon as she saw him she smiled, as if he'd sneaked up behind her, and suddenly she put her hands on his shoulders and kissed him—surprising them both evidently, since she quickly stepped back, stumbling on the hose, and then laughed, glancing at her foot in the dark as he aimed the flashlight there, and said, "It's been a long time."

He might have said the same, but something stopped him. Desire brought along its sharp adviser, who coldly noted how Melissa lost her footing and counseled him to keep his own, to remember that, no matter how young he felt, he was not. A light came on inside and the two of them found themselves looking into a window at Jesse's anxious face peering out. "Oh," Melissa said, a note of remorse, as if she'd been remiss.

When she went in, with Curtis at the door behind her, and said, "Already home?" the boy's face settled into a look of suspicion, not at all what Curtis was expecting.

18

Alice was shaken but determined no one could tell, so, when Little came up looking worried, it seemed a bit presumptuous, that he thought he could see what no one else could, and she informed him she was fine, it was fine, everything was fine. It was true. Cole and Hauser had pummeled her, and pawed her besides, and everyone had laughed, though she guessed that in the confusion no one had seen them grabbing at her, but one thing was clear. She had been mistreated, and with this certainty whatever doubts she'd had about all the other, ambiguous incidents disappeared. As upset as she was, she was relieved to be back in a world she knew well, a mostly benign place with some bad in it, like Hauser and Cole, who had nothing to do with her except coincidence.

At her house she stopped long enough to give some food to the cat she'd adopted—a female, still unnamed, on the assumption that someone would eventually come around to claim her—and to stand in her bedroom a minute and think about changing her clothes. Much as she might have liked to look presentable, when she glanced at herself in the mirror the insult to her uniform, dirt-streaked and scuffed, seemed so telling that she decided to leave it on. Then she got into her car and drove to the brewery.

She'd heard someone say that Frank Johnson was there. The fact that the offices were dark and locked only stopped her for a second while she sorted her thoughts and saw how this, the mere place, didn't really matter. She already knew where Frank Johnson lived. She'd looked up his address after their meeting and remembered it well, since it was on Virginia Street, where she and her friends used to drive now and then and imagine what it was like to be rich and to live in a mansion whose rooms their fantasies could barely furnish. The address, when she found it, was somewhat disappointing, in part because since her high-school days she had lived for a while in a realm more fantastic than anything these people chose to inhabit, in part because Frank Johnson's house was one of the few modest ones on Virginia, newer than the others and smaller. It was at the end of a long drive lined with tall conical evergreen trees, their points like a huge picket fence against the night sky. The house was a two-story sandy-brown brick building, and only when she reached it and looked at the few lighted rooms downstairs did it occur to her that Frank Johnson might have servants or someone else who might answer. However, she was already there, so she went to the door, though she did knock instead of ringing the bell.

She was relieved when he came to the door. Then his look reminded her precisely of her appearance. "Alice?" he said, as if unsure of her name or her presence, she didn't know which.

"I'm sorry," she said, and he said, "No, come in," standing aside so she could.

"I thought I should tell you."

"What? Has something happened?"

The quiet of the house settled on her. The foyer was tiled, cool and dim, a little light creeping into the rooms on either side, catching the edges of a table and chairs in a formal arrangement and giving the whole place a ghostly feel, as if no one quite lived there. As she followed Frank into the living room, where only one lamp was lit and every shadowy thing so orderly, the feeling grew stronger, so that when he said, "Please, sit down," she looked around quickly first. "Now, tell me," he said, still standing. "Have you just come from work?"

"No," she said, "the game, the company softball."

"And?"

"It's not the one thing," she said. "I told you. About the calendar and the poster? There were other things too. But today those same guys, the worst ones, attacked me."

He stared, then he started. "Attacked you?" he said, and he took a step, beginning to turn. "Should we call the police?"

This was not what she wanted, but suddenly she didn't know quite what that was, except that his response was part of it, swift and strong and fitting the way she felt. "I don't think so," she said, "because it wasn't obvious. It was sneaky, it . . ."

"Tell me exactly what happened." When she hesitated, he said, "Are you comfortable? Would you like something to drink?"

She said, "No. I mean, yes, I'm all right, it's just hard to describe. I was trying to steal third base, and they got the ball (one was on second and one was on third), so I couldn't go forward or back, and they kept throwing it, getting closer, and then, instead of tagging me, they smashed up against me, both of them, and while they were like that, with me smashed between, they grabbed me."

Just seeing his frown when she said this, the way a muscle in his jaw twitched, she felt vindicated, and very relieved, because now she could put aside the hard part of telling. "I know it doesn't seem like a big thing," she said.

"When you say they grabbed you . . ."

She looked up at him, waiting. She knew what he meant, but didn't know how to answer.

He said, "Was it sexual in nature? I mean, do you see this as part of a pattern, the pattern beginning with the calendar?"

She admitted it was, sorry now that she'd forced him to ask the question, since it made him turn formal, maybe because he was as uncomfortable with the precise wording as she was. "I thought maybe you could do something," she said. "I mean, without—" She had his close attention again as she searched for the right phrase. "I don't want it to get worse."

He said, "Tell me their names."

"It was Cole and Hauser. I don't know their first names. They're—I don't know—"

Again he waited, listening, but in a way that made her think he must hear something else, a sound she strained to catch herself, until he prodded, low and pressing, "Go on, Alice, they're . . . ?"

"They could overreact," she said. "You know, the way they did last time?"

He was thinking, she could see, and then he smiled. It was strange, like his listening look, distant and intimate at once, as if they'd just concocted a crafty solution together, though she had no idea what it was and felt left out. The whole exchange was quite confusing, tugging on her with the undertow of a secret flirtation.

At last he spoke again. "Was my sister there?"

"I don't think she saw," she said. "I don't know if anybody saw what happened."

"No need to worry her," he said. "You were right to come to me. This might take some finessing, but it'll all work out, and meanwhile I want you to come to me if anything else happens, if anybody bothers you. Anything. You know I mean that."

Persuasive as he was, saying "anything" like a suggestion and searching her face, this was nonetheless it, leaving her nothing to do but go. Still she sat there, uncertain, studying him for a sign. "Are you OK getting home?" he said, and she got up, assuring him she was fine, stopping at the door, just inches away as he opened it for her.

Although her plan, so simple and clear, had gone no further than seeking him out, now it seemed somehow to have gone wrong, and, driving away, she went over each word, every look and gesture, letting them all play out a little longer just to see where they might have led even as she used them to convince herself that she wasn't imagining things. After all, he had reacted just as she had hoped he would, or would have hoped if she'd given it more thought instead of waiting till too late and letting hindsight fix her wishes. In her perplexity and disappointment, she thought of the one person she could talk to and, remembering how he'd been after the game, when she'd put him off, she suddenly felt for him.

19

Alice Reinhart's appearance on his doorstep at ten o'clock so bewildered Little that he stood there staring at her. Coming just as he prepared to go to bed, it seemed to be one of those nonsensical moments his mind often visited on him right before sleep—until she said, "Hi," and woke him up—"Hi," just like that, after how many hours of acting like she barely knew him. He crowded the door and said, trying to get the fact of his bedtime into his tone, "What's up?"

Alice said, "Oh, it's late, I was just . . . ," and took a step back, and immediately he was sorry, aware of her mussed hair and rumpled uniform.

"That's all right," he said, "I was just watching TV—do you want to come in?" and just as suddenly, his incipient pity turned, soured on the thought of what a pushover he was.

Then she said, "I was thinking about after the game, in case you got the wrong impression," so diffident that he started to lean a little, pressing forward, as if to encourage the words along. "After what happened," she said. "You know, with those guys. I wanted to be cool."

Finally he found himself in sympathy with her, because what she was saying was how it had been for him; so he said, "I figured," and he offered her a beer.

When he came out of the kitchen, Alice was standing at the window in his dining room, actually a corner of his kitchen, looking at the neighbor's yard, which was littered with pieces of appliances and broken furniture, all under a cold white light that stayed on till Little didn't know when. Among the debris that resembled a mobile home blown apart by a hurricane and bleached by the years sat the defunct cars, some no more than frames with bucket seats, that the boys in the family worked on at odd hours. "Yeah, it's a junkyard," he said, stepping up behind her, and she laughed in her soft way that made whatever she was thinking seem like a secret. "What?" he said.

"When we lived in New York, the people in the apartment next to ours—it was a big apartment, like a house, actually like a palace—they had a room that looked like that. Some artist did it. It was a sculpture, with a rusted car and a portable toilet and tires, even a broken-down washer or dryer. After we saw it, Alex said, 'See? You can take the white trash out of the country . . .' It *was* kind of homey."

Such a peculiar thing, he started to laugh, but the impulse stopped in his throat. Alice was smiling up at him over her shoulder, as if she had just entrusted him with a small treasure. "Homey?" he said.

"It's like where I lived—I mean, before." Then, toughening a little, sensing a slight, she said, "And you know what, the guys there never would act like those guys today. And if somebody did, they would know what to do."

"But that's where they come from, those guys. They're"— he was about to say "trash," but saw how this might sound, right after she'd claimed to have come from a junkyard herself—"jerks," he said. "For a minute it looked like—I was afraid they were going to maul you."

"They did."

"I mean really."

"So do I." She turned around and looked up at him, as if trying to impress upon him the seriousness of the offense. This, he thought, was the wrong way of looking at it, and it made her position impossible—believing that the rules applied to Cole and Hauser, who had their own, whose idea of an offense was Alice getting in their narrow way. "Why are they doing it?" she said, and he saw that it was worse than he'd imagined; no one could be so naïve.

There was a subtle charge coming off Alice that recircuited anything he might say, channeled it through a fine current of hope. "They're the kind of guys," he started carefully, "who can't admit they're wrong. All of this—this stuff—it's too wrapped up in how they live, what they are, so, if they backed off, it wouldn't be like they made a mistake, it would be like they *were* a mistake."

"They *are*." She set her jaw and looked away, then said, "They can act better."

"That's where you're wrong," he told her. "When you say 'acting better,' that's your idea of how people should act. They'll only act better if somebody makes them."

"Maybe somebody will," she said, still looking off in a defiant way. When she finally turned back to him, something was settled, left wherever she'd been looking, and her interest had a new, curious feel about it. "You know a lot about it, them, I mean."

Implicit in the way she said it, an invisible caress, was her sense of a great distance between him and them.

"I feel like that sometimes. Mad at anyone who gets in my way, or anything, but I see it, usually, that's the thing: I can see it. Mostly I get around it, live with it, whatever. Seeing what's going on makes a big difference."

"You could just say you're a nice guy."

"Would I say that if I was?"

"No, but I would."

She raised herself up on her toes, rested her fingertips on his chest, and administered a kiss. A beer in each hand, he stood as dumbly as he had at the front door, but wildly awake now. As far back as high school, he had been the nice guy girls liked so much though never precisely to this point, and he suspected the same thing was happening. Alice at the moment was merely putting a higher value on niceness, but he didn't mind, not at the moment. He would be as nice as ever. He set down the two beers and put his arms around her slowly, giving her every chance to renege and hoping with his last clear thought that in the thick of it he wouldn't do something stupid out of habit, like saying, "I love you."

20

A night in bed with a pretty, pliable woman made Frank as happy as it might any man, but that satisfaction was nothing compared with the pleasure he found in having denied himself the opportunity, and he had no doubt this was what Alice Reinhart had been offering in her vague, sloe-eyed way. The feeling was not necessarily noble—he was in fact annoyed with himself for finding such a simple person so appealing that his resistance required an effort—but that effort allowed him to put a high gloss of principle on the sense of purpose and accomplishment abstinence gave him.

In this frame of mind, he encountered Melissa at the coffee maker at least an hour earlier than she normally arrived at the office and said in surprise, "Already at it?"

"Already behind," she said. It was such an obvious attempt to put him at ease, perhaps assure him that she wasn't trying to outwork him as well as outrank him, that at once he was suspicious. Now he noticed about her a certain shyness that he associated with happiness, because in her modest way Melissa was always somewhat apologetic about feeling good, and he remembered she'd been playing softball last night and began to imagine her hatching a romance with one of that lot. For Melissa, such an unlikely affair would probably fall under the rubric of noblesse oblige. It was a maddening thought, and as if this showed, she said to him, "Frank?" her anxious tone enough to wake him to how far-fetched the idea really was.

"Did you see the commercial?" he asked her.

"No," she said, "but I heard about it."

"Did you?"

"From Curtis." Since this was all she said, for a moment he found himself searching for significance in it: Heard? Heard what? And why Curtis? What about him, precisely, merited a pause? Their encounter last night at the Greenleaf entered into it. Curtis had spoken to her after that. "Why didn't I know about it?" she said.

He said, "That's a good question."

For no reason except that he'd suggested it, she looked chagrined. She said, "I thought we'd decided—"

"So did I."

"To wait."

For a second she seemed like a chastised child, so he knew that when he told her that, by the way, Dunwitty's tests with focus groups, etc., had been great she would mentally search her desk for a missed report or memo instead of requesting proof. In fact, her troubled look was all he got in answer, a look that nonetheless diluted his satisfaction.

"Actually . . . ," Melissa said. The word sounded like a confession.

"Yes?"

"I've been thinking about the ads. And I came up with something that might— It's an idea anyway. I was going to tell you at a more appropriate time."

"Now's fine."

"In the reading I've been doing, I came across some historical stuff—pamphlets, stories out of papers, there's even an act from the state of Massachusetts, or the colony, whatever it was then, sometime around the Revolutionary War. But they're funny, things promoting beer because it's healthier than liquor—'ardent spirits,' they say. One, the Massachusetts act, I think it was, encourages the manufacture of beer as, I quote, 'an important means of preserving the health of the citizens of this Commonwealth.' Et cetera."

He'd seen that sort of thing. He said as much and waited with transparent patience.

"So. I started seeing a *really* old-fashioned campaign. Corny on purpose—like Bartles & James but different—a kind of tongue-in-cheek thing promoting beer as a healthy beverage along those lines—like an eighteenth-century campaign. There're prints and reproductions in the books, if you want to see them." Although he'd made no comment, she suddenly whisked the whole idea away with a flick of her hand and said, "We can talk about it later," turning even as she spoke. When she reached her door, she cast back a quick smile, shy as her first one this morning.

It was an idea their father would have liked. She had an uncanny knack that always took him by surprise. She knew next to nothing about beer, and yet she seemed to have Gutenbier in her blood, some strange access to the spirit of the company—and even so, she had no notion of it, no awareness like his own. Was her mind really the mess of impressions he imagined it was, or was it merely a matter of style that she wavered and deferred and spoke in her roundabout way, one small aspect of a meticulously plotted approach even more cunning than his own? The question, he supposed, was probably more indicative of his approach than hers.

Recovering some of his earlier spirit, even feeling it whetted a bit against the sense of a possible obstacle, he returned to his office and telephoned Henry and told him to reprimand Cole and Hauser publicly for their misbehavior toward Alice Reinhart. Henry continued to listen long after Frank had finished speaking. Nothing had happened, he finally said, and even if it had, it had happened during a softball game, which even Frank had to admit constituted neutral territory. *This*, he said, was the way to cause real trouble.

"It has always been our policy," Frank said levelly, "not to tolerate offensive behavior. If the policy hasn't been enforced, then more's the pity for anyone who's gotten the wrong idea, because we've had a change of management, as you're well aware, and now we're going to be what you might call vigorous about this. Any offender will be demoted or have his pay docked or, after three incidents, dismissed." He let Henry stew in his refractory silence for a minute before saying to him, confidentially, "I'm sure you see the situation. I'm in a somewhat difficult position at the moment, like you. A matter of adjusting. But let's just say, the tougher the adjustment, the briefer it might be—you see what I mean."

Henry said, "I don't know if I do. Are you saying . . . it's temporary?"

"That depends on how it goes—that's all I'm saying. And, again, things have changed; let's be as clear as possible on that point."

Henry met this with another silence, in which Frank could almost hear the man's mind struggling above the undercurrent—always there, always pressing—of work to be done. "Your sister making things rough for you, Frank?" he said at last.

"Let's just say she's doing her best and leave it at that. I'll tell you what, Henry. Have Cole and Hauser come to my office—now, if you can, I've got meetings all day—and I'll put it to them."

"I can do that," Henry said slowly, "but it's not—now, don't take this wrong, I'm just saying—it might not be the greatest idea—you don't know them's all I mean—to get the guys involved in politics?"

"I'd say they already jumped in headfirst."

It was not until an hour later that Cole and Hauser appeared at his office, the one a squat man with a muscular swagger, the other tall and dark, squared off at the jaw. As he told them what he'd told Henry, embellishing where he could in an attempt to seem both beleaguered and above the whole business, he pictured the incident, saw the woman as he'd seen her last night, pale and supple, caught between these men in a brutish embrace. The image, repulsive as it was, played on and on, exercising a peculiar fascination over him, so that he ceased to see the men as they were before him. Then he found his place again, concluding, and there they were, a look of enlightenment on their grudging faces. Knowing, for them, had a cunning aspect, which he found somewhat alarming, since it only occurred to him now that he had no way of ascertaining what they understood. His alarm was brief, though, assuaged by the very thing that had prompted it: If they were so far beyond the pale of his own character, how much could their thinking matter? He was regarding them—surprised to feel a twinge of sympathy for Alice, whose unfortunate lot it was to work with such men—when his intercom buzzed and Joan announced for all to hear that his sister and Peter Beeksma were waiting.

Melissa had been waiting for a minute when Peter Beeksma came in, shed his jacket, and with a frown looked for a place to put it. Joan lifted the jacket from his raised hand and draped it over the back of her chair, and only then did the man acknowledge Melissa, his one hand flat against his stomach, holding his tie, as he leaned forward, extending the other to shake. "Pleasure," he said; she said, "Same here," and after exchanging a few words about the weather, how hot it was, how dry, so early, they had little left to say and sat side by side on two Naugahyde chairs.

Much as she might have liked to say a bit more, ease the way toward the business ahead, it was Frank's deal. Conscious of the studied ease with which Beeksma sat unmoving, she felt for the first time the power of her position, a subtle thing, how whatever conversation or immediate grace she might be lacking at the moment was more than made up for by her stake in the business that brought the man out. He was someone who had a hand in most of the goings-on in Rensselaer that required boards of trustees or oversight committees or councils of advisers, a man with money and a sense of civic duty composed in large part of a wish to secure and preserve the world that had done him so well. However selfish or unselfish his motives might be, they served the community that was in many ways a wide extension of his personal interests. For many years the president of the region's largest bank, the Mercantile and Agricultural, locally called M & A, he had recently started his own investment firm, identified on its letterhead as a "full-service financial institution." This, word had it, was a predictable success among people who expected him to do with their money what he'd done with his. He had no other way of proceeding than his own, and so he did just that. What he wanted to do now was help his investors acquire a large chunk of Gutenbier, as he himself had been trying to do for at least a decade.

Her brother's office door opened, and two men in Gutenbier uniforms emerged. They were the two who'd been so unpleasant at the softball game, but one of them, the taller, she seemed to know in some other context. This had occurred to her last night and struck her even stronger now, though she still couldn't place him. Simply studying him, she drew a dirty look, quick and cutting, as he passed. She was still following him, wondering, when Peter Beeksma stood up, greeted by her brother, who'd come out of his office with his arms open in a welcoming way he had that seemed to embrace all the world and generally ended with a businesslike handshake. In this grip, the two men hovered above her until Frank finally smiled down, saying, "There you are," and ushered Beeksma into his office, waving her in after them.

That was when it came to her where she'd seen the tall man, Hauser. He'd come into the women's shelter—it must have been five years ago, and he wasn't so gaunt back then, or maybe something else was different—he'd come to collect his wife and children, whose whereabouts nobody was supposed to know, and nobody would've if the woman herself hadn't called him. "Melissa?" Frank said, waiting. The woman, she thought she remembered now, had gone by a different name.

Once she'd sat down next to Beeksma, the two of them facing Frank across his desk like competing interviewees, her brother said, "I've given some thought to what we talked about, and I think we can say, if for any reason the investment doesn't meet your expectations, we—and I'm sure you'll agree, Melissa"—he glanced at her, his manner commanding enough to summon the last of her lagging attention away from Hauser—"we would be prepared to buy back the stock."

"If it doesn't meet our expectations, it may be a bit late for that."

"At the present price."

Without angling a look at him, she could tell Beeksma was staring at Frank just as she was, though no doubt for different reasons. A skeptical minute passed before he asked, "Then why not buy it now?"

"Clearly, we'd prefer to bring in new money instead of leveraging the company to raise it. And let's say we'll be in a better position in a few months, should the need arise."

"Frank," she said, not even knowing how to start, "fill me in, would you? We're not talking about common stock, right?"

Beeksma kept watching her brother as if he, not she, had spoken, and when Frank answered there was some of the same indirection in his tone, as if he and the banker were conversing through her. "The details haven't been worked out," he said.

She said, "But that isn't a detail. Mr. Beeksma, it'll have to be preferred stock, I don't know if that was clear."

He raised his brow at Frank, who considered her for a second or so before suggesting, "You want to protect your position."

"I want to protect the family's position."

"As I said"—again he was speaking to Beeksma— "nothing's finalized."

For the first time, Beeksma turned to her. "Voting?"

"I don't think so." Meaning merely to seem forceful, in hope of hiding how little she knew, she managed to sound snappish instead. She tried to soften her tone. "If Frank's projections are right, I don't see how you can lose. Is this a problem, Mr. Beeksma?"

"Not yet it isn't." He actually seemed amuscd. "Let's look at those projections, Frank."

Something in his tone told her that the meeting, to the extent that it mattered, was over now. While Frank described the prospects for Gutenbier Light, she volunteered a word here and there but mostly sat in silence thinking about what had just been said, which she was afraid (she almost hoped) she must have misunderstood, because she couldn't imagine Frank, conservative as he was, wanting to issue common stock, and could imagine even less—let alone ask him, with Beeksma here, hovering over the figures her brother laid out—where he thought he'd get the money to buy back the stock, especially if it went bust, and was there any other reason for Beeksma to exercise such an option? She wondered why Frank wanted the option there, whether it was really risky, and how it might upset the already tricky balance between their shares—a question that must have occurred to him, though, if it had, the business became that much murkier. Then the banker was standing, dealing out abbreviated handshakes that somehow conveyed the impression that he'd simply dashed in to have a word with an acquaintance and had to dash out, barely pausing when Frank said, "You'll want to attend our next meeting."

She cut in then and told Beeksma, as if she were concurring, "We'll be having one next week." Though this was news to him—necessarily, since she'd just decided—Frank didn't say anything. But as soon as the man was gone, collecting his jacket from Joan without pausing as he passed, her brother turned a look of baffled wonder on her. "What in the hell were you thinking?" he demanded.

"What, did I come on too strong?"

"Too strong? I work my ass off trying to get someone to invest a fortune in the company, and you act like he's out to get us. *We're* trying to get something out of *him*, Melissa. *He* has to be con*vinced*. *That's* the situation."

"I just want to make sure we don't give too much away in the getting."

"Who are you talking to? It's me, Melissa. What, do you

think I'd sell the company short? Or is it—ah," he said, "it *is* me, it's not Gutenbier at all. You think I'd sell *you* short—is that it?"

"That is so . . ." She mouthed the air a minute, unable to find a word for what it was. "Don't we want the same thing?" she said. "I mean, it's not the terms I—How am I supposed to know? I didn't know about the commercial, did I?"

"Apparently not," he said, with the same tempered incredulity she'd seen on his face earlier, although since then she'd gone over every slip and snippet of pertinent information she possessed and had nearly convinced herself that she couldn't possibly have known, which made her brother's expression that much stranger.

"What, are you saying I should've?" Just pronouncing the words embarrassed her, an answer of sorts, but too late to stop them. Frank seemed to know, and said nothing. She managed a chagrined smile, he returned a meagerly forgiving one, and she withdrew feeling better in an atmospheric way, as if the exchange had been a bit of bad weather passing between them.

She went back to her office by way of the coffee maker, slowing as she passed Curtis Niemand's door, which was standing open. With one hand on the jamb, her impression of simply passing by, she told him, "I'm scheduling a board meeting next week."

He said, "Do tell. Was that Peter Beeksma I saw?"

She glanced down the hall at Frank's office, then returned to Curtis to find him looking amused at her stealth. "Perhaps you'd better step in," he suggested, a mock conspirator, then laughed outright when she closed the door behind her.

"I don't want Frank thinking we're in cahoots," she said.

"God forbid."

In cahoots, she thought; was there something in it? But there was no telling what his dry expression meant, so, becoming more self-conscious by the minute, she told him about the meeting between her and Frank and the banker.

"Shouldn't I have been in on that?"

"I would say so, but," she said, "with the way the vote went, and"—she made a helpless gesture—"everything, I don't want Frank to think—"

"What is Frank thinking, precisely?"

As she told him how the meeting had gone, she saw in his frown the very concern she had felt, and felt guilty about having, and now was dismayed, even offended, to see reflected in Curtis's face. With quick conviction she asserted, "Frank would never issue common stock."

"I should hope not. Unless he's got some notion of getting his hands on it—though you'd have the same opportunity, of course. To buy a proportional share. Assuming you have the means." His look converted this last remark into a question, which, when she hesitated, he made explicit. "How are you fixed for money? Ready money."

Again she hesitated, embarrassed. "I could always use more."

"Price still doing your books?"

This was her father's accountant. "Right now he's doing the estate stuff."

"Does Frank know your situation?"

"Boy," she said. "You two."

"Us two? You don't mean Frank and me?"

"A couple of paranoids."

"With two significant differences. First, whereas Frank may in fact be paranoid, I'm only justly concerned. And, second, Frank's concerned about himself, while my concern is for you."

The way he was watching her, as if through the thicket of his words, seemed to give an undertow to what he said. He proceeded to talk—about dividends and par, present margins and percentages, her position, Frank's—and the feeling persisted. In fact, it was all she could recall with any certainty when she went back to her office and tried to make sense of the rest.

22

It was during a meeting about the new beer that Graves gave his speech, and Little was slow to attend. Alice's first words on waking were, "I'm late," her movements matching in their quick efficiency. Even her smile was efficient—economical, as if to show him that she was not the same languorous girl he'd gone to bed with, as if he might not understand that a person could feel different at midnight and at dawn, a warning note in every brisk maneuver she made getting dressed, suddenly his buddy with a cautionary edge. Instantly he'd told himself that if she'd woken up all cuddly and clingy he might just have been alarmed, but the thought wasn't consoling, was in fact so unconsoling that he guessed that was all the thought was supposed to be, because *he* felt the same this morning as he had last night, remembering how it was to have someone there, to touch and talk to and take care of, to wake up to. Instead, then, he told himself to be careful, temper his expectations for the moment, because, however dubious the moment seemed, there might still be something in it for him if he could be smart. Much as he wanted something better and could tell the feeling had somehow fixed on an improbable woman, he wasn't indifferent to the prospect of simply getting laid. After last night, after such a long stretch of sinking into celibacy as a sort of second nature, this really seemed, on second thought, a worthy pursuit.

His prospects diminished somewhat when Graves handed out the new assignments. Because of the increased production for the first big brew of the light beer, they were going to triple shifts next week, and Alice would be adding nights, while he would be doubling, mostly days. At first he assumed this was what she got for being new, but then Graves came to Hauser, Cole, Walt, and Steve, all senior and all on the graveyard shift, and whatever logic lay behind the assignments disappeared, as some grumbling among the ranks attested.

There followed Graves's gruff version of a pep talk. The next few weeks would be tough, he told them, but they would be making brewing history. Because the supervisor tended to run on, Little eased up listening. One minute Graves was going on about how big this was, what he expected, typical talk while the crew rumbled along at a lower frequency, and the next thing Little knew, the room was utterly silent. "I've said it before," Graves was saying then, "tell me, folks, does this sound familiar? We won't put up—and when I say 'we' you know who I mean—we won't put up with that sort of behavior—not at the plant and not on the field, and when you play softball you're still Gutenbier, and we're calling that the first infraction for both of you. One more, and it'll come out of your paycheck. Two more, and you're looking at severance pay."

This was about Cole and Hauser, Little would've known even if he hadn't been at the game, since the two of them, standing across from him, were like some kind of anti-magnet, repelling every eye in the room. Graves said, "What can I say, boys—oh, excuse me, and girls—we're under new management, and we aim to please. If we don't look good, then they don't look good, and we don't want that. All we want is a plant that's running as smooth as our beer, and any boulders in the path of progress are gonna be crushed. *Comprendes?*"

Little sickened to hear this. The assignments—most of them, anyway—were punishments after all, and if he could see this, so could Cole and Hauser, and it would only make them mad—not in the grumpy way they might have been about drawing the late shift, but purposefully so, with some-one to blame. The first thing he thought of was asking to be put on late nights himself, but then he saw how this might look to Alice, like a pathetic ploy to be around her, or, maybe worse, like what it was, proof he thought she needed looking out for and he was the one who ought to do it.

He did try to say something to her. He managed to get next to her leaving the locker room, but just as he started to speak, she smiled just short of smug and said to him, "So there."

Immediately he looked around to make sure nobody could hear. "What?" he said. She cocked her head quizzically, as if bemused that he could be so slow. "What?" he asked her. "You think that settles it?"

"Don't you?"

"What if it doesn't?"

"They're fired," she said, so clear on this point in Graves's speech that Little's question obviously puzzled her.

"After last night," Little said, and her gaze quickly floated away, "I mean at the game—after that—I don't know if it's over so easy."

When her eyes returned to him they were still somehow looking elsewhere, wherever she'd shunted his silly concern, so he said, "How about working nights?"

At this she perked up. "I'll be doing lots more."

"How do you figure?"

"It's fewer people, isn't it? Doing the same thing. I'll get way ahead of where I am. I mean, my place in the line."

"That's possible," he said, and as she edged away, her smile drifting off again, he was left standing there, facing a long day of work superimposed with a picture of Alice lying back, arch-ing up, spreading her legs, that might as well have been a figment of his fantasy.

23

After visiting his daughter and granddaughter—already a toddler—for the half-hour he set aside every Saturday, Curtis Niemand drove by Francis's house on a hunch. Seeing Melissa's car there, with Frank's Saab parked right behind it like a hulking bug, he pulled up alongside the entrance. He knocked, assumed they didn't hear—the maid was not here on the weekends anymore—and let himself in.

In the study he found Melissa sitting on the Persian rug right where it was worn, where he'd seen her sitting countless times before, crosslegged as now, her golden face tilted back as if her father's words were light, though this time she was listening to Frank, who was standing over her, looking for all the world like a defeated lover, a weary grimness in his posture and the way he stared over his sister's head as he spoke until, interrupted, he turned with a look of annoyance that cleared as soon as he saw who it was. Melissa's smile was welcoming but vaguely apologetic, as if she thought she should get up and greet him but didn't have the wherewithal. In her palm, resting curled on her crossed legs, she held a pair of spectacles.

"I was just going," Frank announced and, sharp as a reporter with the story, flipped shut a spiral-bound notepad he'd been holding. His name issued from his sister as a note of protest. With the sound, and his abrupt movement, the room was suddenly so altered that Curtis felt he might have broken a spell.

"If I'm interrupting . . . ," he said.

Frank flicked away the suggestion. "As I said, I was just going." He stooped and plucked the glasses from Melissa's hand and put them on a book lying facedown on the table next to Francis's old reading chair. "And just in time." His fingers lingered on the spectacles, now in their customary place. "My sister's getting sentimental."

"The glasses," Melissa explained, and Curtis looked again at the threadbare wingback that, after so many years of sitting, still held an impression of Francis. The book was *Captain Sir Richard Francis Burton,* by Edward Rice, one he'd been waiting to borrow.

Briskly Frank glanced around, administering the look like a last touch, and then, as if it had just occurred to him, said to his sister, "You're not going to sell the house?"

"I'm holding it in trust for Jesse."

"It must cost a fortune."

"The property taxes. Otherwise there's only Abel and Mrs. Carpenter. I thought about closing it up, but I hate to put them out. And, you know, everything would go to seed."

"What about living here?"

There was a certain nonchalance to his voice, casual testing, that Curtis could see register in Melissa's uncertain smile.

"It doesn't seem . . ." At a loss, she tipped her hand.

"What it seems is foolish to keep two houses."

"Would you want to live here?"

"Oh no, I hate it." He cocked a quick smile at Curtis and elaborated. "Like living in a model, you know. Everywhere you look, a frozen lesson in the way you're supposed to live— *one's* supposed to live—and so"—he frowned around, made a sweep with his notepad—"so much of it. Much too much for me."

"It is big," Melissa conceded, as if encouraging him.

Frank nodded, then turned to go. Melissa shifted as if to rise, Curtis offered her a hand, and she followed her brother out of the room.

Trailing them, Curtis found the two standing as if in line at the sideboard in the parlor, Melissa behind Frank as he deposited into his folded arm a number of objects. In the crook of his elbow he had already a packet of envelopes bound with a cracked rubber band, and on this he stacked a small leather-jacketed journal, an opal necklace and a cameo brooch, a pair of yellowing gloves with a pearl at the wrist, a photograph in a folding gold frame—all of them possessions of his mother's that Curtis recognized from the last sorting of personal effects after a death in the family. Francis had insisted that he, Curtis, of all people, should help him put his wife's things in some semblance of order, which, once Francis had lifted and examined each item with all the perplexed delicacy of a skeptic handling religious relics, had turned out to be precisely the order in which they'd been found. Cradling his collection, Frank turned to his sister and raised his eyebrows, his fingers laid along the edges of the letters at the bottom of the pile. She said, "I wouldn't burn them," and as she added, in a conciliatory way, "yet," he said, "I know. Curtis."

"Frank." Curtis smiled at the military politeness of the exchange.

As soon as he was gone, an air of intimacy seemed to settle over Curtis and Melissa. "Burn them?" he said, and was aware of murmuring, although they were alone.

"My father's letters to my mother." Melissa wandered past him, back into the study. "I didn't remember them ever being apart. But Frank knew. Even one bunch from the Korean War. Before we were born." She was facing the wall of books, but even from behind, the tilt of her head expressed bemusement. "He wanted to burn them. Because they're 'personal.' " This apparently bewildered her even more. "And all those things. They're all my mother's. You know, it's sad to say it, but he never got along with her."

"Maybe in his heart of hearts."

"They were both so stubborn. So alike. Like they had a patent on it and the other was infringing."

She was silent for a moment, still considering the books. "So many familiar faces," he said, looking with her, then touched the open volume by Francis's chair. "I was waiting to borrow this one."

She turned and lowered a look on it, blinked, and said, "Oh, take it. Take whatever books you want. My father would've wanted that."

"That may be a bit freehanded of you. In your capacity as executrix." Though he said this lightly, she seemed disconcerted, so he added, "I have most of these myself. Many of them anyway."

More than anything, the smell of the room affected him. It already had the whiff of history, perhaps nostalgia, about it, the warm must of so many old volumes, the seasoned wood and leather and the ages of dust in the drapes and rugs and furniture, which still breathed ever so faintly the aroma of the cigarettes Francis had once smoked. Melissa stooped to run her hand along the top of the frayed set of the *Encyclopaedia Britannica*. As she rose, her fingertips trailed over the familiar books—European history and Antarctic exploration, Russian novels, Winston Churchill, William Shirer, the Van Loons— each a marker of a certain time in his friendship with Francis, each, for Melissa, a moment she'd interrupted, she told him now, how she would come into the study, respect her father's silence for as many seconds as she could, then tell him something, anything, inconsequential, and he would respond, "Look at me, Melissa. This is what I call a good example," and go back to his book.

"We loved him," Curtis allowed. "But he could be a horse's ass."

Melissa emitted a startled laugh.

He pulled out *The Fountainhead* and said, "Remember this?"

"*The Fountainhead*?"

"You used to hover around when we talked about books, on the margins, always doing something else, you know, but it was obvious—once Francis pointed it out—you were listening, studying what we said like a little spy, and soon enough—sure enough—in a week or two, you'd venture an opinion on whatever book it was."

Her smile was wistful, wandering back. "I guess the thing about being young is, you don't know you're transparent."

"I might have said 'translucent.' " Until then he'd only been half aware—sensing in the modulation of his voice, the tempering of his gaze whenever she looked at him—that he was negotiating a seduction, but now he concentrated the full force of his attention on this possibility, summoned into one long look all the commanding power of the memories conjured by the moment and the room. "Then," he said, "he started doing it on purpose." He considered her, suggested softly, "But you knew that."

"Actually . . . " She turned back to the books, her wondering frown last to move, as if it were weighted to him. She touched the spine of one book. "You mean like this?" *The Brothers Karamazov.*

"Precisely. You must have been all of thirteen. Even your father was amazed when you plowed through that one in a week."

"What about *The Fountainhead*?" She was like that girl again, regarding him, waiting to learn, but this time without the pretense of already knowing. "It doesn't seem like something—"

"That's how it struck me too. Which may be why I remember so well. But you were—what?—fifteen or sixteen, and he'd come to think, in typical Francis fashion, that you had your head too much in the clouds. So Ayn Rand was supposed to bring you down to earth. Or something. By way of a counterbalance? Instill the capitalist principle."

Incredulous, Melissa was looking not quite at him, but past him, at some point in her own history as it assumed a new shape. "God," she said, "it worked."

He lowered his head to look into her eyes. "We all liked that book when we were sixteen."

As if to keep the emerging picture of her past intact, she covered her eyes. Curtis moved her hand. "I suppose nobody likes to be manipulated," he said. "But his intentions were always benevolent."

"And yours? Did you have any intentions?"

"I was an adult, remember. Opaque even to myself."

He knew as well as she did that this wasn't true, remembered exactly when, with his hands just so, he'd seen himself reflected in her warm expression and understood that it was incumbent on him, as an adult, to stop this. It had been so many years since he'd seen that willing look in anyone he'd wanted that for a long moment he savored it, feeling her tentative surrender in his fingertips as they traveled down her neck, along her shoulders, slipped around her arms, and finally gathered her in. "But now?" He smiled and bent his head to kiss her, murmured smiling against her cheek, "Now I think I see it."

He took his time about kissing her again, conscious of her stillness in his arms, and then her hands crept up his back and pressed him closer, and in a sudden single-minded moment of desire his every thought fixed on logistics, how to move her next, when she whispered, "Should we go upstairs?"

Lightfooted, like a girl sneaking him in, she led the way, took him up into a room he'd never seen, sat down on the modest bed, with its pale-blue quilt, and, placing her hands on either side of her, lifted her face as if it were purely her will that he do whatever he wanted. Already his mind was so far ahead of him, seeing her supine, open to his touch, that the actual, practical problem she presented—from the tiny buttons down her shirt to the probable intransigent bra to the mechanics of removing his pants while maintaining whatever it was about him (it could hardly be dignity, but maybe the illusion of it, the romance in how she saw him) whatever kept her looking up at him like that—the practicalities, like a trick sprung on his slower, unsuspecting body, rendered him immobile, until her eyes faltered for an anxious second. Instinct, bidding him hurry, swept aside the difficulties, and everything swiftly followed just as he'd foreseen it, with no distinction between the imagining and the doing and no idea how exactly she'd come to be naked under him, shimmying the narrow bed away from the blue wall.

24

Alice's shift was over at midnight, and she walked home, thrilling a little to the feel of it, herself out alone at night and not afraid of being nabbed or mugged or murdered. It was possible that there was danger abroad even here, but Rensselaer, with its cool air and rich nighttime smell, was so different from the New York she'd mostly imagined from the inside and above, her tower in the castle, so real whereas New York was mostly a nightmare, that the idea of danger had become as distant and unreal as the city, somehow more unsettling to contemplate—so she mainly didn't and gave every stranger she encountered more credit than might be due him. The newness of her life now was far from wearing off, and in the way she went about it she was a bit, she believed, like a girl going off to college, an experience she'd missed but was determined to recoup in a singular way, the confidence of having eluded Alex standing in for the brashness of eighteen. Pleased as she was to be learning her job, every small success she acquired seemed to open a view of a whole world of jobs she might succeed in. Now that she believed she'd made a friend of Mary, who just tonight had told her all manner of intimate things about her struggles with her teenage daughter, she could see a field of friends spreading out before her too. She remembered to count Little among these, the fact that she'd slept with him receding already into the realm of youthful error.

It was in this benign state that she unlocked her house,

walked in, and tripped over something. For a second she stood where she was, perplexed, listening to the silence, same as ever, and toeing the obstruction. It was one of her boxes. The overhead light had no bulb, so in the darkness of the curtained living room she felt her way to the one working lamp, encountering obstacles with every few steps. When she reached under the shade to turn the little knob, her fingers brushed the bulb, and it was warm. This preoccupied her for a second as she absorbed what the light revealed—disorder everywhere, the room ransacked. The furnishings, the old owner's spindly things, were as they'd been, but all the cardboard boxes she had stacked in lieu of unpacking were scattered, opened, many of them toppled with their contents spilling out.

Her stumbling progress had prepared her for something—a surprise, and probably unpleasant—and in view of what she found, her first thought was of Alex. It struck her like retribution for imagining she could escape him, and for the next two or three minutes, as she made her way around, examining the mess, sneaking looks this way and that before each move, he seemed to be everywhere. But then, when he didn't appear and she got a better look at the way her belongings were strewn about, Alex began to seem less and less likely as a culprit.

There were her clothes, cast out in a swirl from box after box: the silky underthings and slinky garments that she didn't wear anymore but kept on some cautious impulse, the whole box of camisoles and teddies and tap pants emptied in a whirl of colors; another tipped to make a cascade of shoes, the shiny pumps in every shade, their pointed toes and spike heels interlocked like a crazy puzzle.

It occurred to her that someone could be in the house. Already well inside herself, shrinking from the alien touch of the chaos, she simply froze and waited for a sound, and as she did, the suspense easing with every silent second, her thoughts circled back to Alex. Only minutes earlier, she'd been feeling safe as she had never felt with him, but now, it was a curious thing, she found that the very same circumstances made her feel unsafe, cut loose, among strangers. Why, she couldn't help wondering, *hadn't* there been so much as a word, a sign? Never once had she believed he wouldn't miss her, wouldn't—however mad, however wronged he felt, or even righteous in his weird way—seek her out and try to make her see so-called reason. For an instant her conviction about the way he wanted her, a measure she had made some use of, turned into a question.

All this she dismissed as shock as soon as she understood it and meanwhile had concluded that no one was there. Her relief made room for her to feel how shaken she was. Wading through her undergarments, a garter dragging at her ankle, she shivered inside her uniform, although she knew it was hot here. It always was, like a steamy hothouse maintained to preserve the old lady who had lived here and had left behind her musty lavender scent, and her lamps with shades like Easter bonnets, and her tiny round tables on one leg with three feet, even her afghans in pink and brown. What had seemed homey and welcoming only eight hours ago began to look strange and ominous, waiting or decaying, she didn't know which, but infected with death either way. She bent and sifted through a heap of clothing at her feet. A charmeuse kimono hung from her hand, and suddenly the thought of someone else's fingers touching the same fabric filled her with revulsion and she dropped the thing. The first touch of nausea stirring her stomach, she picked her way through the mess. Before her, the desk stood out as a safe haven, the papers and books somehow less susceptible to the filth that clung to every soft thing flung around. But when, in a slow and methodical way, she began to make stacks of the bills and cards and keepsakes culled from the jumble on the floor, these things also became strange in her hands. It was like looking at her own obituary in the making, all the documentation of her life rifled and cast off as trash, and she found herself thinking her way into a stranger's mind, imagining what it all might reveal.

The nausea was rising in her throat when she noticed the yearbook opened to her picture and at the same time heard a muffled mewing. The cat—she looked around for her. For a second, there was no sound. Then another soft meow came from the desk, and she opened the drawer, and the cat leapt out, so furious in her scramble for freedom that she grazed Alice's arm with her claws. As Alice tried to catch her, the cat scampered away and slunk in a circle just shy of her reach.

Blinking back tears, she looked at the drawer from which the cat had emerged. That was where she'd put photographs Alex had taken, pictures he liked her to pose for wearing funny little outfits and collars and cuffs that his shop sold. They were the only things she'd stolen when she left (though "stolen" was not entirely true, since they were pictures of her) and the first things she'd put away, buried where they belonged, under all the stuff that added up to a better image of her. Now she went to the drawer and rooted through the letters and programs and clippings of haircuts from *Glamour* and *Mademoiselle*, heartened to find some of high school still there, in order, tossing these things out on the floor with the rest of the refuse as it became clear they hadn't been disturbed—and there were the photographs, squared to the corner, untouched.

All the while, her mind was working on the problem of what had happened, and why, and who'd done it. Gazing at the pictures, she felt for an instant exactly that queasy feeling the calendar gave her, and all her fear and suspicion fixed on the men who went with it, the sensation just like being pinned between them for that endless minute on the softball field. Her whole house closed around her with the same sickening pressure. Her breath coming hard, she panted to get out, but stayed for a minute, laboring, where she was. She picked up the photographs and tore them into tiny pieces, which she carried to the sink and fired with the matches from the stove.

The smoke and the acrid smell choked her, but no more than her disgust. How she hated Alex—so much, so abruptly that it overwhelmed her—for putting her in this position, and then, as if he were the problem, sorting through her mind for its solution, her thoughts arrived at Frank Johnson as he'd been in his doorway, looking at her so sincerely and saying, *Anything.*

It didn't occur to her until she heard his muted voice that it was after midnight and he might be sleeping. His silence when she told him what had happened worked on her nerves, and she was more aware of the time than before, of the peaceful quiet that she'd interrupted, the distant security of his big house and his life, so she told him it had been Cole and Hauser, the ones he said he would take care of. What had started as a suspicion a minute earlier made such sense that it already verged on conviction. Now, though, hearing herself say it, she knew she was trying to convince Frank Johnson that she'd been right to call, nothing more, and she wavered, which was the last bit of uncertainty she could stand. At once all the trouble they'd caused her crowded into her mind, and it was not long before her motives were lost in the crush, and with them any subtle distinction between what she felt and what she knew for a fact.

He said, "Have you called the police?"

"No," she said.

"Do."

For a few seconds, stumped by the prospect and the questions it prompted, she didn't say anything. Was she, for instance, supposed to implicate Cole and Hauser? Or did he want her to keep anything about Gutenbier out of it? Maybe, she thought, this was his way of saying she had become too much trouble for him. At last she asked him, "What should I say?"

This seemed to puzzle him almost as much—at least, he

didn't say anything for a while himself. Then, in a tone that explained—it was so obvious—he told her to say exactly what had happened, just what she'd told him. He was sorry, he said, the warmth of his voice so soothing to her jangled nerves that for a minute she thought she would cry, and he really wished he could be there to help her but knew she could see why it would be better if he stayed out of it. "But if you need me . . . ," he said, and the promise hung there until she managed to tell him it was OK.

She was more confused after this call than before, but the sickness in her stomach had been replaced by another, fluttering sort. She could see, he had said, and she probably could've if he'd said a bit more, and that was what she kept coming back to while she waited for the police, how few words there were, with so much understood—or so much she was supposed to understand, which might even be better.

25

He'd almost gotten back to sleep, or so he told himself, when he heard her car and found himself wide awake hoping the noise hadn't woken his neighbors. For an hour and a half, he'd been lying in bed going over their conversation, if it could be called that. What troubled him most, at least on the slippery surface his thoughts were negotiating, was his failure to ask her how she'd known who'd broken into her house. "I think," she had said, as far as he was able to recall now. *I think it was them* was what he was fairly certain she'd said, though if she'd said *I think*, a comforting thought, he couldn't imagine he wouldn't have asked her why. The omission implied that no explanation was needed—and that implication was damning indeed. It was also a nuance, necessarily subtle, and look how unsubtle the woman's mind was, he tried to reassure himself, but at once he was subjected to a mental picture of her as she'd sat before him on the sofa, face tilted up, all eyes, looking not so much unsubtle, let alone stupid, as young, much younger than she could possibly be.

The look impressed itself on his conscience, which so far his thoughts had managed to skate over, and irritably he searched around until he got hold of another reasonable idea: she was a victim of coincidence; her suspicions were unfounded, accusations false. He could see her as she'd sounded, holding the phone like a lifeline, whispering about the wreck around her as if the room might hear, that look of hers wandering with no one to fix on now—and whereas the image had provoked him only a minute before, now it filled him with sympathy utterly unlike the earlier, needling kind. It was a surprisingly powerful feeling, seductive as any sexual fantasy, and he sank into its depths.

The harsh coughing sound of her car then, disrupting his drift toward sleep as well as the fancy that buoyed him along, was too crudely real, like an angelic vision in a silent picture opening her mouth to emit a Bronx rasp.

He'd pulled on his slacks and his shirt and was about to go down when he realized that she hadn't knocked yet, or rung. Stopping to look out the window, he found that Alice hadn't even gotten out of her car. There was something about this, the dark little car sitting there like a troubling second thought, that erased the last traces of his annoyance, even quickened his step descending.

When he opened the door, she opened hers, then sat there still and silent as if awaiting a sign from him. Finally he was forced to go out to her, the cool grass, then pavement, under his bare feet a peculiar sensation, as if he hadn't touched ground for years—and it occurred to him that he probably hadn't—and rounding the car with the lush smell of the air weighing on him was like walking into a memory of no particular time and place, a long-ago lifetime of warm summer nights. "Alice?" he said. He bent with his hand on the frame of her door. "Are you all right?"

"I—" she said, and he thought she was going to say, "I'm sorry," as she had the last time, but even this much seemed beyond her now. Taking the hand he offered, she let him help her out of her car, limp as a puppet. There was something sensual in her abstraction, as if she'd materialized from his musing but not completely, not until he drew her farther. It was at this juncture, with his hand on her arm as he started to guide her to the house, that he became aware of a sort of stupor overtaking him and knew he could shake it off, and should, and tried, to the extent of asking her, "Did you call the police?" Hearing his own voice, so low that it slipped right under what he said, he cleared his throat and stopped and looked at her with as much authority as he could muster. This, however, was just where the danger lay, so, when her expression flickered and her soft yes came out a question, he was moved to reassure her.

The tenderness that swept him was predatory in its force, overwhelming caution, every practical consideration except the most immediate, which was next to nothing. Her uniform. He kissed her, his hand already tugging free her shirttails, sliding up her sides, then down again, into her pants, so he could sink his grasping fingers into her. Her adjustment as he did this, the way she curved to meet his hand, spurred him past impatience, and he let go long enough to lead her to the living room, although he only made it as far as the rug before he started again to undress her and pull her down.

The hard nap of the tapestry on his knees afterward was the first reminder of how rash he'd been. Lying there, her clothes open but not removed, Alice gazed up at him and smiled timidly, as questioning as ever and looking for all the world like the helpless innocent he'd imagined, although his dream of mastery looked just as pathetic now, with him here on his knees, waiting for the proper moment and precisely the right words to tell her that this wasn't what it seemed.

26

This would be the first she'd seen of Curtis since Saturday, though they'd spoken; he'd called her that night, when she'd gone home to Jesse, then again on Sunday, before she'd even had a chance to get into a quandary over what came next, who said what, how much, and when. Now, about to conduct her first board meeting and with so many things to think about, she found herself thinking about him instead, whether she should sit by him, how to act. She was just trying to dismiss this as too silly, mortifying if someone of Curtis's poise only knew, when she noticed that no one was taking the seat to her left anyway—the only empty seat when Curtis came in—and he sat there, naturally, smiling as if without a second thought. In a muddle of chagrin and satisfaction, she glanced around the room.

It was full to overflowing, with so many extras present that the heat they generated seemed to temper the overconditioned air. One of Curtis's junior partners, here to represent the firm's investment-law department, had wriggled in between her and Frank. Peter Beeksma had brought his "team," and on the other side of Frank another crew assembled, Randy Gold's, all of them, like a chorus line, leaning at precisely the same angle as their leader as he spoke into her brother's ear. Henry was here, and Martin, an array of bottled beer on the table before him, which, with the quizzical, slightly anxious look he kept shifting about, gave him the unhappy air of having misunderstood the occasion. Only the two cousins were missing.

As she started to speak, Curtis tapped her leg under the table, a hello, and in her surprise she croaked a single note. Quickly she cleared her throat and, smiling—at everyone, all looking at her now, and only covertly at Curtis—suggested that they begin without Ernest and Francis, who'd surely be there any minute. She introduced Peter Beeksma and his contingent, then Randy Gold and his. Uttering nothing but formalities so far, she was aware of Curtis at her side, of how every insubstantial word she said drifted his way, acquiring a certain weight from his attentive presence. Then she saw Frank focusing on Curtis too, in that keen, assessing way of his that always made her feel found out and now gave her the eerie feeling that he'd sensed Curtis's fleeting touch under the table. She stole a sidelong look, but Curtis was turned away, unaware, watching Martin pour beer into pilsner glasses at the far end of the table—and when she returned to Frank, his eyes were on her.

Gratefully she accepted the first glass from Martin, then waited for the rest to be distributed before she took a sip. The beer was dry, mildly hoppy, with a pinpoint effervescence, disconcerting at first, that she'd only slowly come to like. "Well?" she said, but it was in the nature of the ritual that no one would say a word until she announced her verdict, predictable as that pronouncement might be, since the meeting wouldn't have been called unless the principals had approved the new beer. Still, Frank was watching her intently. "I think it's perfect," she said, but his attention held, as if there must be more. Instead, having no idea, she turned to Martin and talked with him, for the benefit of all, about the peculiarities of the brew, how long it had aged, and, specifically, his concerns over the barley crop, which wouldn't be the same after such a dry season and might alter the taste of the beer.

Again she solicited the others' reactions, and this time they complied with enthusiasm. "I admit it," she confessed, "I was afraid it would be thin. But for a light beer, it's—"

"Not light?" Henry volunteered, and she laughed—but he didn't.

"I wouldn't go that far. Compared to the classic, it's a breeze. Nice color, Martin." She raised her glass to him. "OK, let's try the others."

One by one they sampled the other brands. Although at such an early hour they merely took sips, their general satisfaction produced a somewhat inebrious air, and, buoyed on it, Melissa announced that she'd been rethinking the ads, only to feel the company's spirit flatten in a sudden silence.

Everyone, beginning with Henry and Martin, turned to look at Frank. He steepled his fingertips and over their point considered her, the shadow of a smile darkening his face. "Shall we assume we've reached the marketing portion of the program?"

"Yes," she said, "I guess we have." Momentarily the room seemed to narrow to the two of them, her and her brother, the rest a dim gallery, until, with a barely perceptible shift, Curtis reappeared on the periphery, a sharp presence. She said, "I've had some feedback on the ad and it's confirmed a few of my own concerns, about preserving our identity, especially competing in such a glutted market with our limited means—I mean, for a company our size, it might make sense to take a different angle. And then there's the risk of losing old customers, losing our base."

"The point," Frank said, speaking with all the patience of a television father, "is to expand our base. It's not the old customers we're after. It's the new ones, the buyers in number who could do something about our 'limited means.' I don't really see what this has to do with our standard."

"It's all Gutenbier, Frank."

She winced at the conciliatory note in her own voice. Curtis stepped in when Frank asked her what kind of feedback, exactly, she was talking about. "I know what Melissa means," he said, "having heard a bit myself. Women who'd drink a light beer if it didn't insult their dignity."

At this Henry snorted. "Dignity," he muttered incredulously, his outburst so unexpected that it surprised a laugh out of some of the others, and Frank absorbed their amusement into his benevolent expression. "Henry's right," he said. "We're not going to sell much beer by appealing to people's dignity. As for feedback, I've got some for you, in the form of orders." He opened a folder that had been lying in front of him and extracted a stack of papers, which he proceeded to pass around the table. Everybody took a copy gratefully and fastened on it. Then, one by one, as each glanced up and found Frank regarding Peter Beeksma, they all focused on the banker, who seemed genuinely engrossed in the document, oblivious to the rest of them. "Impressive figures," he remarked before looking up at Frank, who smiled with the barest hint of a nod. Presumably prompted by this exchange, Curtis nudged her under the table, but she didn't know what to do, how to regain the meeting's momentum.

Impatient, with herself as much as anyone, she pulled her knee away from his. "You don't think this had anything to do with the drought we're having?" she said, flipping through the sheets Frank had handed out. "Where are the figures on the standard?" She explained to the table at large, "*All* the orders are way up."

"So nobody's too offended?" Frank suggested—and that was when the cousins, so late she'd forgotten them, finally appeared. They rushed through the door, flushed with hurry and the heat, and stopped as if they'd run flat into a cold front. Certain he had everyone's attention, Francis waggled a newspaper at them. "Have you seen this?" He laid it on the table with a flourish, like last-minute evidence.

"Yes," Henry said. "That's a paper."

"That's right," Francis answered sharply, "tonight's."

Curtis picked up the paper and held it so he and Melissa could read the folded front page, where the words GUTEN-BIER WORKER stood out as if spotlit in a headline. There was Sue's byline—and there had been two calls from her this morning, unreturned because of too much work waiting but resounding now, low and dull, as she read about a break-in at the house of an employee, Alice Reinhart, that girl from the game—an act of vandalism that the article said, in the paper's characteristic unaccountable way, was "suspected to be" part of a pattern of harassment being conducted at the Gutenbier plant. Disoriented for an instant, Melissa reread the line, then looked to the right, where a big red box framed a list of examples, bulleted, of the insults Alice Reinhart had sustained. Her disbelief gave way to dismay as she reached the parenthetical instructions under one item: "For contents of poster see page 2"—just as the paper erupted, like a clap waking her from a trance, although it was nothing but Curtis turning the page.

"Does anyone know anything about this?" she asked, but of course no one else knew yet what "this" was. Frank reached across the table and relieved Curtis of the paper, open now to a list of reasons why "Beer Is Better Than Women." It might have been the weather, the glance he gave it was so cursory, and then he flipped back to the front-page story. The others watched him, the cousins especially avid about the effect of their find, as he skimmed the copy, folded the paper again, and handed it to Curtis, saying, "Let's nip this in the bud." Like a father reviewing the news at the breakfast table, he summarized its import for his waiting family. "One of our employees has accused two of her co-workers of vandalizing her house, after some other incidents at the plant. You know something about this, Henry?"

Like someone under oath but not quite sure how much it covered, the supervisor scanned the faces suddenly turned to him before venturing, "Not about any vandalizing."

"We'll look into it," Frank said, by way of concluding the business, and, picking up his report again, was just about to resume when Beeksma asked, "Is there a question of liability?"

"We're amply insured," Frank told him, then, with a nod at the newspaper Curtis held, which seemed to have mesmerized every eye at the table, "Despite the sound and fury, it seems a bit far-fetched—wouldn't you say, Curtis?"

"I wouldn't say a word just yet."

"Good policy."

A look passed between them that, no matter how tense it was, denoted agreement and nettled Melissa. When Curtis knocked knees with her again, seeking a subtle acknowledgment of she didn't know what, she kept perfectly still, observing her brother as she tried to puzzle out the situation with what little information she possessed. The meeting proceeded without her, halting only momentarily, as at a curiosity, when she interrupted Frank's overview of Beeksma's offer to ask Henry to have this woman, Alice Reinhart, come to her office after they were through, and then when she broke in again to tell him, on second thought, to send Joe Martin, the one they called Little, first.

27

It was like being summoned to the principal's office, nerve-racking no matter how good you'd been (because who ever knew?), but as soon as he got there his apprehension gave way to a sudden brotherly concern. Small as she was behind her big desk and with that uncertain expression, she didn't look much like a boss, though in an instant he observed that she sounded like one, that, even saying a nothing like, "Joe, I hope I didn't interrupt anything," as she did now, her cool clear voice intimated certainty, namely the certainty that somebody would listen. Because there was no good answer—either she'd interrupted or he'd been doing nothing—he shrugged agreeably.

She slid a folded newspaper toward him and, tapping an item outlined in red, said, "I don't want to put you on the spot." Immediately he was uncomfortable again. "But the other day," she said, "at the game? You seemed to be implying something, so what I want to know, before I talk to Alice Reinhart—is there anything to this? Anything you know?"

While she talked he was reading, seeing what it was just as she spoke Alice's name. When he could no longer credibly pretend to be reading, he pulled down a frown and cast it around the room in an approximation of searching thought. This too could be sustained only so long, so he finally nodded in the general direction of the article. "The calendar was there," he said. "And it's true Alice didn't like it, so I took it down."

"You—"

"I know her from high school," he explained.

"And did one of these"—Melissa Johnson touched Hauser's name where it was printed in the paper, then moved her fingertip to Cole's—"did they put it up?"

Again he shrugged, or started to, since as he sank into his shoulders he glanced up and saw in her disappointed expression that in trying to be noncommittal he had come across as dull and stubborn. "I really don't know," he told her. "When Graves said his bit about—here's what happened—after I threw it away, it was there again, on the wall, and Alice took it down that time, only Graves saw her do it. So he talked about it—to the crew—said to stop it, you know, and then he handed it to Hauser, but that could mean anything."

"And the other things?"

"I only know what Alice told me."

"OK," she said, "that's a start. What did Alice tell you?"

"Just what's here. Not the house thing. That's a new one." Just thinking about it, actually thinking for the first time since he'd read it, he felt his anger flare—inexplicably, at Alice.

"You didn't see any of it?"

He shook his head deliberately.

"When Graves, Henry, talked about it?"

"I don't remember word for word." And then, because she looked so skeptical, he said in Graves's behalf, "He docked Hauser a day's pay."

Her doubt turned to disbelief and then suspicion, which seemed to fix on him, unfair as that was, and all she said, weakly, was, "He did?"

"Yeah." Helpfully he added, "After the softball game he talked about the policy, where anyone who . . . does something gets docked, and after three times, they're fired."

At this Melissa Johnson opened her mouth to speak and closed it, though not all the way, without saying anything. At last she asked nonchalantly, "Does my brother know about this?"

"This?"

"The incidents. The punishment. The policy?"

"I don't really know that either."

He'd only gotten halfway through his answer before she was moving around the desk, subtly conveying that she was walking him to the door—and he was glad to go, although he had the peculiar sense of having told her more than he even knew enough to hide, let alone reveal.

28

Was he lurking or aflutter? Hard to say. Either way, not himself, Curtis managed to be at the coffee maker pouring out a cup when Melissa emerged, happened to see him, waited until she caught his eye, then beckoned. Surreptitiously he took stock of the man she'd just ushered out, a uniformed employee, large and muscular almost to the point of hulking, perhaps one of the newsmakers, although his big wide face seemed more boyish than brutish. "One of the culprits?" Curtis said anyway, reaching her, and raised his steaming cup, a toast. "Two beers isn't my idea of breakfast."

"No," she said as she hurried him in and closed the door, her ardor ironing the lurking and flutter out of him and returning the man of substance, who stood husbanding his reserves, only to be brought up short when she said, "Can we fire them?"

He took a moment to adjust. "The alleged perpetrators?" he said. "Yes. And they can sue us." Her pretty brow puckered with exasperation and he suppressed a bubble of indulgence, went on with unmoved reason. "Unless we know they did it."

"What about those other things? How much do we have to know?"

"Proof would help."

"Someone's word won't do?"

"You mean a witness?"

As if she hadn't heard him, or hadn't asked in the first place, she said, "Do you—are you aware of any policy we have about this? I mean, anything explicit. An explicit policy."

"Aside from the civil code?"

Again, in her preoccupation, she couldn't spare a second to acknowledge his response—or him. In fact, he might as well be watching her from behind a mirror as she stared unseeing—until a knock startled her, and she blinked and focused on him for one sharp instant.

"Come in," she called, and a woman he'd seen, a redhead, the one who'd shown up at Francis's wake in uniform, peeked into the office. "Come in," Melissa had to say again before the woman would comply, edging around the door. At a glance from Melissa—a signal, he assumed—he settled in to stay, but with the casual air of sitting out an interruption.

Whether his nonchalance was remarkably effective or simply unnecessary, the woman made no distinction between him and every other fascinating fixture of Melissa's office, which she examined in the quizzical manner of someone transported to a strange place in her sleep. "I was sorry to read about the trouble at your house," Melissa said. Alice Reinhart interrupted her survey just long enough to acknowledge the remark with a quick tilt of her head toward her shoulder, her eyebrows raised as if to say, *Yes, it's too bad, isn't it?* "I'm sorrier to say this is the first I've heard of any trouble you've had here."

Now the woman gazed directly at her, and in the face of her innocent and patient interest, Melissa looked briefly disoriented. Her voice flagged uncertainly as she asked, "Did you report any of these incidents to anyone?" At this the other woman's expression went so vacant, like the open face of a foreigner awaiting translation, that Curtis found himself viewing her as he might a natural phenomenon and only emerged from his reverie when Melissa said, "I can't do anything about a problem I don't know about."

Alice blinked. She squinted deeply for a second, then offered diffidently, "Henry Graves knew about it."

Melissa sat a few seconds considering. Then she inched forward one cautious question after another until a picture of the supervisor's bungling began to take shape, and what a sorry shape, worse than arbitrary. Curtis went on listening in silence, no longer bothering to feign indifference now that the women were so engrossed, the wide-eyed Alice staring spellbound at the mere fact of Melissa's full attention, while Melissa became more absorbed in the story, which drew him in as well, so that it was with a peculiar satisfaction, as at a ringing denouement, that he heard her pose the question: "And my brother?"

At the mention of Frank, Alice put on a thinking expression, pinched and embellished with a slight squint—such an obvious evasion to a veteran lawyer that he was a minute or more speculating about what she might be hiding before he managed to remember that this woman wasn't the guilty party, which only made her reticence that much more intriguing. At last, though, her memory produced a fragment: "I told him some of it. I think that's why Henry . . ."

Melissa looked stricken. The woman must have noticed too, because she quickly added, as if to explain away a possible slight, "I met him when I started working here, so he seemed like the one to talk to."

"Of course," Melissa murmured, "how could you know?" Curtis wondered how to make sense of Alice's remark in view of her behavior—and Frank's—at the funeral, whether Melissa remembered, had even noticed at the time. In this way, he reckoned, any number of insignificant coincidences could begin to seem significant. Meanwhile, Melissa was soberly trying to convey the spirit of Gutenbier to the woman, telling her in all earnestness that this was a family business in more than one sense, that workers and management here had a tradition of looking out for each other, and that their employees' safety and comfort was a priority, so she hoped Alice would help them and trust them to rectify this unacceptable and truly anomalous situation.

What the woman's reaction was he couldn't tell, because she listened so agreeably, was so earnest herself, and left without comment, her quiet, obliging demeanor making Melissa's speech, which he knew carried every conviction, sound like so much talk. It was, after all, what anybody might say—and probably should say, under the circumstances. For a moment he said nothing. Although Alice Reinhart had gone, a trace of her attention, a subtle charge, hung in the air, something erotic, an implicit longing—or perhaps he was just filtering the woman's presence along with everything else through the fumes of his overheated mind, which hadn't been in such a state since the most feverish days of adolescence. Now he found himself wondering what sort of mood the exchange had evoked in Melissa, who was looking so reflective, and whether it might serve his suit.

For all his speculation and calculations, he'd reached no conclusion, except to say something limp but leading, like "Well . . . ," when the intercom buzzed, the door opened a crack, and Sue Newhouse appeared just as the speaker on Melissa's desk announced her by name. Whereas the other had looked timid peering in just so, this one looked wary— and seemed confirmed in her suspicions when her searchlight gaze stopped on him: "You again."

"None other."

Immediately she dropped him and fastened on Melissa, asserting somewhat aggressively, "I tried calling you this morning."

"What, to alert me? I read it."

"No, to get your comment."

"What a bunch of crap. That's my comment."

"It's 'crap'?" Sue Newhouse handled the word delicately. "Is that for the record?" She monitored Melissa in a guarded, tentative way, as she might a sleepwalker courting danger unaware. Melissa burst out in a pained voice, "How could you write such a distorted piece . . ."

She didn't finish, but her friend continued to listen, then said, as gingerly as before, "It's distorted? So you know something about it? And, just to set the record straight, you want to say . . ."

"No, I don't. Or I didn't—know it—till I read it in the paper. Which hardly seems like the best way to . . ." Again her voice trailed off, and again the other waited a safe interval before speaking.

"As I said, I tried to call."

"This morning?" Melissa rifled through the clutter on her desk, producing a few pink message slips, which she held up fanned out like tickets for sale. "When does the paper go to press?"

Now the woman shunted a cautious look Curtis's way as she eased a step closer to Melissa's desk. "Melissa," she said, lowering her pitch and casting one last leery glance at him, "it makes a good story, it's true, there's no question about that, but between you and me—it's—I can't see this happening on your watch. You know what? It is crap. And the thing is, you know it. It's not something happening in the paper. It's not about *me*."

"Where'd you get it, then, the story?"

"Police blotter. Same as every Saturday night. Talked to the desk sergeant, talked to the victim." She opened her hands, *voilà*.

Here Curtis cut in: "So you got your information from Alice Reinhart?"

"No, the police got their information from Alice Reinhart, and then she fleshed it out for me. What's your point?"

He glanced at Melissa, encountered her gaze, and though it was coincidence, at most an acknowledgment, the reporter noted it; he felt her interest shift, invest the insignificant glance with all the meaning it might have held. Somewhat wary of her, he started to excuse himself, speaking of waiting work, but she was closer to the door and, with her new insight, more determined to bow out. She said to Melissa, "I just wanted you to know."

"I knew," Melissa said. "I knew enough. Now're you going to tell our story—our side? I mean, anything besides Alice Reinhart's . . . complaints?"

"Wouldn't that be a flagrant conflict of interest?"

They both stared, struck by her nerve. "Why?" Melissa said at last.

And he said, "You mean because of your involvement with the late owner?"

He might have been mistaken, but she seemed to flush. "See? Just mention the idea and I'm in trouble." With that and a hasty mumbled something about later, she was out the door. When he turned, Melissa was neatening the mess on her desk, squaring the pink message slips she'd brandished at Sue. He sat down in the chair in front of her.

"So," he said. "Frank knew."

Her nod was slow and sidelong, a concession. "But I don't know what I would've done differently."

Still she hadn't raised her eyes. He waited and, when she didn't, prompted her: "You don't."

"Henry could've handled it a little better, but—look—he did something. The guys were punished. There's this policy. The only thing Frank didn't do is tell me, and"—she smiled up at him ruefully—"that's so Frank."

"So Frank and so unfrank," he said. "Frank is so unfrank."

"It's like the ads," she insisted. "He wants to take care of everything himself. Partly to help, I mean, because he should—or just to spare me—and partly to show everyone: He's not beside the point."

"Not hardly." Seeing her shrink, sink ever so slightly under his sarcastic tone, he tried to lighten it, reached out to catch her curled fingers in his palm, and said, "Oh no, not the soft spot."

She didn't smile, but didn't move her fingers either. He

folded his hand around hers, and at her answering grasp leaned in to administer a chaste kiss to her forehead, and then stood, able to speak of business that needed attending to, though he found he couldn't fix his thoughts on a single pressing task in all the legal world.

29

He had little call to visit the plant during working hours but did so whenever a reason arose—as now, when Beeksma requested a tour—always with the sense of exercising his prerogative as master of everything here. It wasn't a sense he had of himself but one that was pressed on him, conveyed in the workers' careful, checking glances as he passed, an impressing on him of his place.

Every tour he made recalled those he'd taken as a boy, bobbing in his father's wake as all the warmth in the cool brewery closed around him—all the smiles and expressions of interest, so different from any he'd encountered since. It seemed the place itself had changed, and all the people in it, when in fact more than a few of the workers he saw now were the very ones who had smiled on him then. That this remembered atmosphere was a certain order of grace conferred not on a boss, however beloved, but on a father with his small son in tow did occur to him now and again—only dimly, though, because he could hardly make out the difference in himself, let alone imagine he'd once been adorable. He could hardly conceive that somewhere along the line coming here had become tantamount to being loved, so instead he made sense of the warmth by telling himself it was actually his love of the place, heightened, admittedly, with a touch of nostalgia.

Like a lover, he was subject to the brewery's moods: the turgid, aromatic heat around the mash kettle; the briskness upstairs, where the barley was ground; the cool, biscuity waiting air of the aging cellar. With Beeksma attending, listening with a smile of polite interest as his eyes made a ceaseless inventory, he felt each room adopt a stolid, businesslike mien more suited to the banker's cast of mind than his own.

They had just come to the foot of the mash kettle as the wort was being pumped back from the lauter tun when, in the middle of explaining the process, his hand raised to point, Frank looked up and found himself squarely in the sights of two men on the catwalk that circled the kettle. In an instant he recognized Cole and Hauser. They were standing side by side, hands on the rail, gazing down at him like a couple departing on a cruise. Their lofty attention, discovered like that, discomfited him. For the first time in his experience, the towering room around him assumed a forbidding aspect, and he felt Beeksma staring at him too, until he remembered that he'd broken off in the middle of saying something, his hand in the air. With a wave of his raised hand, dismissing some annoyance he wasn't inclined to explain, he proposed that they move on to the bottling plant, across the alley.

The racket there offered reprieve. The atmosphere matched his agitated mood. The workers, each intent on a task and sensibly muffled with the requisite goggles and earplugs and hat, didn't turn to stare as he shouted to Beeksma about the functions of the various machines, confident the man wouldn't raise his voice as far as he'd have to to interrupt.

They'd nearly reached the end of the line, and he was explaining the Filtec machine, which scanned the cans for any that had been short-filled, when the worker who'd been monitoring the operation rose and ceded his place to Alice Reinhart. For a few seconds the man stood behind her, hovering as if she were not his replacement but his guest. She paid him no notice, nor anyone else, simply settled at once into watching the screen where the cylindrical X-rays kept marching along. There was that raptness about her, in the angle at which she was leaning to look and her utter indifference to the man at her back, that he found fascinated him in part because it mystified him that anything, especially so mundane, cast that kind of spell.

He hadn't been thinking of her, hadn't been looking, hadn't necessarily wanted to see her, but now, as she continued to sit there so still, suspended while everything around her moved, he felt his relief that he'd escaped her notice giving way to pique; images of her disheveled, regarding him in that same rapt way, replaced the neat figure before him. He was stirred out of his erotic reverie by Beeksma, who was trying to ask him something—something, it alarmed him to realize, that concerned Alice.

He led the way out of the noise. Once they had the window between them and the bottle house, Beeksma asked, "Is that the one?"

The question was startling, as if, all the while he'd seen Beeksma as immune to the nuances in the air the brewery breathed, the man had actually been conducting his own intuitive tour. But another look at Beeksma, who was waiting with a curious patience that seemed not the least bit enlightened, disabused him, and he remembered the newspaper, which everyone at the meeting had seen. "I believe so," he said.

Through the glass, Beeksma was examining Alice as if her person might offer an explanation, or a solution. All he said then was, "Hunh."

30

This was what Little noticed as he left the bottle house for lunch, Frank and another man in office gear, peering through the window at Alice while they traded comments, like scientists monitoring a lab experiment. He couldn't hear whatever it was they were saying, and by the time he'd taken out his earplugs they'd stopped talking.

Since Melissa Johnson had shown him the story, he'd been trying to keep an eye on Alice too. There was something disturbing about getting the news secondhand like that, not disturbing in the way the incident itself was, or its implications, which Alice obviously didn't see or she wouldn't have named Cole and Hauser, but disturbing nonetheless—proof of her misguided trust, her faith in processes over people, and questionable processes at that. The newspaper? If there was a worse way to manage those two, he didn't know of it. They were bullies, bigger than the playground variety but otherwise the same, and all a person could do was ignore them or smash them. Being in the news would blow them up larger than life, and then what? The uncertainty, as he saw it, was far more worrisome than their predictable petty behavior. And if they *hadn't* done it (in the story, Hauser's wife said they'd been playing cards in her kitchen all night Saturday), their appearance in the paper was only that much riskier.

And there was something else. Outside of what he'd learned from Melissa Johnson, he hadn't heard a word about this, not a whisper, which gave him the same uneasy feeling he'd gotten watching Frank Johnson watch Alice, as if it were all part of an experiment he was conducting.

The thought was so outlandish, Little checked himself and took a look around and shortly came back to what he'd been thinking, but from a better angle. If Alice was fascinated with Frank Johnson, or whatever she was with him, he was hardly to blame, nice as it might be to blame him. It wasn't the man's fault that he had so much more to offer than Little could ever even dream of matching, and if Alice couldn't or wouldn't see that the offer just wasn't open to her, that wasn't Frank Johnson's fault either.

Arriving at the lounge, Little found himself looking at something stuck to Alice's locker. With a glance over his shoulder, he eased the thing, a folded magazine page, out of the locker vent. Even from the door he'd thought he could make out a breast, and now that he unfolded the paper a nude woman confronted him, fleshy, clad only in pearls and high heels, and strangely familiar. Dismay rose in his throat as he turned the page over. It was torn from a magazine he'd discovered as a kid, one picture from a whole photo spread of a girl who looked so much like Alice Reinhart that he'd been fooled for a long time. It was, in a way, what had gotten him started with Alice, and seeing it now brought back those days with a sweetness he wasn't sure they'd ever had. On top of that, he couldn't help seeing what he'd had no reason to realize at seventeen—the girl in the picture, whoever she was, was so young, it had to be a crime. She was holding her breasts, half showing them, half hiding, and anyone could tell that she wasn't even fully grown. At the thought of somebody pawing over this young girl who might've been Alice, a queasy feeling came over him, and then he heard footsteps and flattened the page against himself. As soon as he did it he knew he'd done it too fast, just the kind of move to make anyone curious. Holding the paper to his chest like an oath, he hunched and pretended to work at his bootlace, but Chuck was already beside him, saying, "Whatcha got there?" No faster trying to come up with an explanation, he said, "Nothing," which really piqued Chuck, who reached, demanding to see, and ripped the picture.

Little was left with the lower half while Chuck studied the girl's face and torso and remarked in a tone of proud wonder, "I went out with her."

"No you didn't," Little told him. "It's not what you think."

"And she wouldn't even let me get to first base. Second base. Whatever it is, where you feel 'em up."

"That's not her," Little said. "It's someone's idea of a joke. Give me that," and he swiped the torn page out of Chuck's hand and crumpled it into his pocket.

Chuck stood there blinking like a dog tricked out of its toy. "What?" he said sullenly. "I was just looking."

People were starting to come in, so Little shouldered past him, muttering, "It's not her." His urgency impressed itself on Chuck, who watched him all the way to his locker. He'd just opened it when Hauser appeared, and he leaned in, farther than he had to to extract his lunch bag. With a sidelong glance he noted how Hauser looked directly at Alice's locker, then scanned the room as nonchalantly as somebody suspecting a prank.

It was half an hour later when Alice showed up for lunch. Sitting there, going at his sandwich and banana like one more job he had to finish, Little had been thinking about the situation—Alice's situation but his too, now that he'd been such a clod. He was inclined to think that the page had come from Alice's, for instance, since in his mind the magazine began and ended with her, but if he was going to be reasonable he had to concede that there'd been other copies and this picture could have come from any of them. Reason, however, was not very workable against the charm of such a singular, personal relic, and, the further he got from its rigors, the stronger his conviction became. Reason aside, he would say he was certain of where the page had come from and from whom.

What to do about it was less clear. If it was evidence, then surely he should give it to someone—a prospect he didn't like to consider, in view of the confusion over who the girl was. Of course, he could sidestep the confusion by giving the page back to Alice, but there was no foreseeing how that would turn out. It might frighten her into being more careful. Or it might make her mad, with an opposite, even disastrous, effect. She might expect some sort of explanation (or, worse, action) from him. Finally, if he did nothing with it, there was just a chance that nothing would happen. That might be the end of it.

He'd come to this point—which, because he'd been stuck there a while, was beginning to feel like a resolution—when Alice walked in, chatting with Mary. Right behind them were Hauser and Cole, back from wherever they'd taken their lunch. Seeing them, Little stood, the motion so steep and sudden that he stared back in surprise when they all looked at him. Next he found himself in front of Alice, saying her name in a peculiarly hearty manner that bulged out like padding against Cole and Hauser. Mary was watching and Alice looked mildly pained, but he persisted. "When's your break?"

"Four-thirty," she said.

She spoke cautiously, but he rolled on, flattening his pride and perhaps his last hope of ever seeing her soften again. "Let's have a drink then," he said. "OK?"

He pretended not to notice how long she hesitated, or how she answered when she finally did, with a shrug, saying, "Sure," as he knew she would, for the very same reason she didn't want to, a certain delicacy.

Just then, Henry's voice broke over them, barking "Reinhart!" like a command. "Pay phone!" he said, and she responded with such alacrity that Little could feel the wake of her relief slapping him where he stood.

He turned to go. Hauser and Cole, for whom he'd mounted the performance, were already on their way out the door.

31

When Lillian Roth had suggested they might want to talk, Alice couldn't bring herself to admit whatever it was she might be admitting if she were to ask why. The lawyer sounded like a voice from PBS. So Alice had simply agreed, curious but not surprised anymore to find herself wanted. Lately she was in demand, which she took as a sign of progress of some sort, although what sort wasn't so easily surmised, since everybody's interest in her seemed to have a different meaning—Frank Johnson's, for instance; his sister's; that reporter's; Cole's and Hauser's; and this lawyer's—and she'd forgotten Little, who was probably standing on the steps to the brewery right now waiting for her. He would probably wait for a long enough time to squeeze another concession from her, persistent in the way she was forgetful, patient as he was way back when nobody would've guessed he was anything besides a pest.

It was a good thing he could wait, because she was nearing the lawyer's address, and she had other, more pressing claims to consider. There was what, in her brief talk with Lillian Roth, she had come to think of as her case, which would be so much clearer if she at least knew where Frank Johnson stood. What would he think if Lillian Roth wanted to represent her, go against Cole and Hauser, or even Gutenbier? As sympathetic as he'd seemed, and determined to do something, Frank Johnson was still the boss, and even in the grip of romance a man was partial to his own business. That he was in the grip of romance was obvious to her, if not to him. She hadn't seen it right away herself, when what was much more obvious was how sorry he was about what had happened, and that had distracted her awhile, until she began to see what it really meant. If he was so sorry, then he wanted her more than he didn't, more than whatever went against her in his mind. In his hurry to have her, he had lost the struggle he was having with himself. There might be some time now while he told himself it was all her doing, but that wouldn't satisfy him for long, boss that he was, and soon enough he would go back to wondering: Had he really given in? He would have to test himself again; and if he'd given in once, he would a second time, and a third, and so on, until he had to tell himself that this was actually what he'd intended all along.

She could help him work his will into line with his wishes, if only she knew why he thought he shouldn't want her, whether it was anything she could change or maybe persuade him to ignore. For a while, in his sister's office, it had seemed quite hopeless. Melissa Johnson summed up everything she didn't have, not just because she was rich, though that was a good part of it, probably the source. It was in the way she talked, the way she looked at you, even the way she moved—like she belonged and the belonging ran so deep she didn't have to think about it. You wouldn't find her rolling around on a rug in the middle of the night with a man she barely knew. It seemed so unfair that the woman could have that air even though she had a kid with no father around. And somehow that only made her more appealing. Leaving her office, Alice for one minute imagined going home with Frank, except that Frank was somewhere in the background of the picture that emerged, his sister the hostess of the daydream, beckoning and patting the seat next to her—an image that fled almost at once, as far as the distance Melissa Johnson's gaze had seemed to cross every time she looked at her. She wasn't even snobby, just so wrapped up in the difference that she probably didn't see it, and that was most unfair of all. Now Alice found the thought of Frank reassuring, since there was no difference that sex couldn't bridge, and in this respect surely she had the advantage.

This swell of confidence swept her into 301 Seventh Street, Burnham & Locke, and deposited her at the desk of a handsome young man whose high cheekbones, marcelled hair, and spectacles perched on his nose like a prop reminded her of so many of Alex's models. Regarding her for an instant over his glasses, he asked her name as if it were a matter of great delicacy, led her into a room with a table and chairs in the middle and nothing else, and said, "Lil'll be right with you."

The assurance that had seen her in ebbed while she waited, until she felt as stranded as she did at the doctor's, a feeling the lawyer's appearance didn't do much to dispel. Lillian Roth was tall with short white hair and eyes that already seemed to be making a diagnosis. "Alice?" she said, leaning closer to shake hands. Alice noticed now that she was beautiful, in her severe way, without makeup or jewelry or a hairstyle to bring it out. When she went on to ask, "How are you?" Alice couldn't imagine saying anything but "fine." And when she said, "As you probably gathered from our conversation on the phone . . ." Alice tensed, suddenly suspecting that she should have gathered more. "I'm interested in what's been happening at Gutenbier," the woman said. "Particularly to you. If everything I read in the *News-Trib* is accurate, you have grounds, ample grounds, for filing a complaint. I'm guessing you've considered that."

Not wanting to admit she hadn't, Alice tipped her head as if she were considering it even now. "I wouldn't know," she said at last. "Those guys . . ." She frowned at the disturbing prospect they presented.

"I was thinking the brewery."

"I don't know. I think it's just those two guys."

"Two guys, OK, let's—" Lillian looked around like a

schoolteacher trying to come up with a better example. "Hold on," she said. "Why don't we go in my office."

Every surface in her office was piled with papers, files, and books—except a chair facing the desk, which she vaguely indicated before sitting down herself. On the desk, next to an ashtray, an air purifier whirred. Lillian pulled a folded newspaper out of a stack of stuffed paper-organizers. "Now." She pinpointed a passage with her long, narrow finger. "This poster you found in your locker? What did you do when you found it?"

"I took it to Frank Johnson. He's the boss."

"Yes, one of them—and?"

"He called the supervisor, Henry Graves, and told him to dock whoever did it a day's pay."

"You knew who did it?"

"I could guess."

"But you didn't tell Frank Johnson?"

"No."

"So either Frank or Henry Graves knew who'd done it?" Lillian made a note.

"Probably Henry Graves," Alice ventured, watching the lawyer's hand. When it made no move to write, she looked up and found herself framed in Lillian's gaze. "If you tell a lawyer something . . . ?"

"It's strictly confidential. If the lawyer in question happens to be your lawyer. But you'll have to make a decision about that eventually."

"But this . . . ?"

"Consider it a consultation."

Emboldened, Alice asked, "Would it be the same as suing, filing a complaint?"

"It could come to that. It all depends on what kind of determination—or ruling—we get on the merits of the case. If it even comes to that. You might, for instance, want to explore administrative remedies before going to court. That's the preferred course. But if you opt out of the state process and sue in federal court, the stakes are higher, quite a bit. It's all in what you're after. What you're trying to prove, and what you're willing to risk."

Alice's perplexity must have been apparent, because Lillian quickly said, "We're getting ahead of ourselves here." They would, she said, go into all of this in detail, process and procedures, once she had a clearer understanding of the situation. There was a form that asked the pertinent questions, but she preferred to ask a few of her own first—if Alice was willing?

Once she realized that Lillian was waiting for an answer, Alice managed a modest shrug. All right, then, next, Lillian said, she wanted to know about the calendar.

Because this turned the discussion away from Frank, Alice felt easier at once and started trying to describe exactly what had happened, telling it in her painstaking way, sparing of words when she wasn't sure, until she got to the calendar's second appearance and told about taking it down, and Lillian raised her eyes from her notebook and said with some surprise, "You did?"

It wasn't something she'd thought much about, except at the moment, but now, prompted by the lawyer's tone, she reconsidered it and was somewhat impressed herself. As she went on she found herself warming to the subject, calling up the words she needed with an ease that surprised her. She discovered that she remembered the incident in minute detail, right down to the very words Henry Graves had uttered, which she repeated now, extrapolating from the feeling they had given her to the impression they might make on someone as discriminating as Lillian Roth. It wasn't a doctor she resembled after all. Lillian Roth was really more like a teacher, the kind who balanced severity and sympathy so precisely that meeting her standards became the supreme accomplishment. Alice hurried to tell her about how Henry Graves had handed the calendar to Hauser. Her momentum carried her into an accounting of other insults—being sprayed in the holding tank, grabbed at the game—but midway her enthusiasm started to flag, until, when she reached the point of describing herself squeezed between Cole and Hauser, she faltered, embarrassed. What she saw now was the scene as a laughable spectacle, herself in the middle, the way it must have looked to anyone else, and she heard the laughing all around the field. It drowned out her voice. She fumbled for some way of telling about Hauser's fingers smashing her breast that wouldn't make her look foolish, not just on the field but here in this office, in front of this woman, to whom such things would never happen.

Lillian had stopped taking notes and was sitting there contemplating her like a discipline problem, her head propped on the heel of her hand. Slowly, like a sleeper, she laid her other hand on her own breast in what Alice believed, for one baffled instant, was a reenactment and then saw that the woman was simply feeling for her cigarettes. She left the pack in her pocket once she'd ascertained its presence.

"Perfect," she pronounced at last, expressionless, and Alice smiled uncertainly. Then Lillian focused a swift, sympathetic look on her, as if she'd been neglectful. "We won't let the cavemen go," she said. "But I'd say the later model merits more of our attention." She went on to say that "specimens" like Cole and Hauser had to be dealt with, but they couldn't do their dirty work unless someone let them. The whole system was flawed. Had Alice seen Gutenbier's new commercials?

First, she said, they should be clear about their terms. Working one paper, then another, from her jammed organizer and sliding them toward Alice, a fingertip tapping a passage or two in each before the next page covered it, she explained the state and federal definitions of sexual harassment. What interested her most, she said, and what interested Alice, was something that occurred under both statutes—the creation of a hostile or offensive working environment through unwelcome sexual conduct, which, she hardly needed to add, was what they had here. She pointed out a paragraph in one statute and, as if reading with her finger, scanned the words until she came to what she wanted, then stopped with an emphatic tap. Alice read the word "permitting" but no more, because Lillian was moving her hand again.

What Gutenbier was doing, she told Alice, was considerably more aggressive than *permitting*—which brought her back to the commercials. They reflected a certain sensibility, but, what was worse, they encouraged a certain sort of behavior, the very sort of behavior Alice was objecting to.

Alice in fact hadn't seen the commercials, had only heard about them, but what she'd heard about seemed unrelated to what had happened to her. There were the calendar girls and the girls in the commercials, but how were they any different from half the women on TV? She was trying to frame this as a question without sounding critical or revealing her ignorance when Lillian, as if she could read even this in Alice's carefully composed face, conceded that what Gutenbier was doing wasn't really any worse than what any number of other companies produced, but they were close at hand—in her backyard, as it were—and the lateness of their entry into this sick sort of race might suggest that they weren't hardened to it. They might just be susceptible to moral suasion. They were certainly susceptible to legal influence, and she believed that she could make a case that behavior like Cole's and Hauser's was a natural and predictable consequence of the attitude reflected in, encouraged in, promoted in their marketing.

There was something stirring in the way she sounded this last note, a positive charge that registered with Alice as a challenge, compelling but intimidating in the manner of patriotic speeches, rousing in her the conviction and the wish to act without a corresponding sense of what to do.

"What do you say?" Lillian said.

Alice said nothing, hoping the woman would help her by

guessing the answer. What she guessed, though, was not really helpful. "If you're uncertain," she said, "take your time. I don't want to push you into anything. And I certainly don't want to pursue this unless you're one hundred percent committed to seeing it through. You should know, this won't make things any easier for you at Gutenbier, although I don't see how they could get much worse. And my hope is, it would make things better in the long run, not just for you, but for any woman who works there. Speaking of which: If you'll give me the names of a few of the others, the women you work with, I'll see if they want to join you in the complaint. We can manage without them, but they'd improve our case."

"I don't think they have any problems," Alice said.

"Maybe they're simply not saying—it's not hard to imagine, in view of the response you got. And whether they're saying or not, that calendar, the poster, the ads—those are problems they're having. I should say too, assuming we go ahead with this and we're successful—and I have no reason to doubt we would be—you wouldn't have to work there anymore."

"But I want to work there."

"Even better. That way there's no mistaking your motives. So you'll give it some thought?"

"Could you tell me how it would go?" Alice said. "I mean, what happens first and everything, what I'd have to do."

"Certainly," Lillian said, and her pleased smile, as if this were the start of an agreement, made Alice begin to hope it was too. It occurred to her that she should talk to Frank Johnson about this. But already she was telling herself she wouldn't, would just wait; it was only strategic in a romantic sense.

32

At Losers, Little took a stool between two men he knew and bought them beers. He hadn't really expected Alice to show, he told himself, only hoped she would so he could prove that he had other business with her than what she must think. But what she thought was obviously enough to keep her away, and he couldn't blame her—since she didn't know what he had in mind, or maybe she did, better than he knew himself. Now, though, he couldn't fool himself about Alice's grudging interest: grudging had gotten the upper hand. And with this certainty, he didn't have to worry any longer about what to do, since there couldn't be any question about his motives anymore.

However many beers he'd had, they put him on the queasy side of elation, a state he could almost believe was atmospheric as he walked through the warm, heavy air dense with the brewery's yeasty smell. Passing his own house, he paused just long enough to consider cleaning up, but when a maudlin inner voice asked, "Why bother?" he went on. His neighbors, welding something in the spotlight, looked up through a fountain of blue sparks and waved.

Alice was slow answering his knock. He scanned the windows, sure she was peeking from one, but there was no movement. When she came to the door, she had a cat tucked awkwardly under her arm. She stopped and it struggled, squirmed out of her grasp, and fled down the walk. "Kitty," Alice called softly after it, "Here, kitty." Finally she looked at

Little. "Sorry I didn't meet you," she said. "That call I got, it was for an appointment, I forgot to tell you."

"There's appointments, and there's appointments," he said. "This'll just take a minute."

She hesitated. A wave of irritation almost overwhelmed him, but his wish to disabuse her wouldn't let him walk away—a good thing too, because once she'd stepped aside he saw that this might not've been another slight. Her house was a wreck, tipped boxes everywhere, with all her belongings tumbled out and strewn across the floor, all shadowy except for one small clearing in the middle of the mess, a floor lamp casting a yellow cone of light on an armchair where Alice must've been sitting. If he needed any more encouragement, this was it. He took the crumpled pieces of paper out of his pocket, rubbed them smooth as best he could between his thumb and fingers, and held them out to her.

She looked at them but didn't take them from him. He stood there waiting, watching her face as her eyes wandered off the page in his hand and came to rest on nothing he could see. "How did you . . . ," she said. "I thought . . ." At last she raised her eyes to meet his and sighed, "Oh, Little."

"It was on your locker," he said.

She was still staring at him, an eerie, almost sad look on her face, not at all what he'd expected. "I told you that wasn't me," she said.

Now he was starting to become impatient, because there was only so much help a man could offer where he wasn't wanted. "I know that," he said. "It might be evidence." He reached for her hand to try to make her take the torn pictures, but she snatched it away from his touch with such force that she fell back a step.

"Evidence?" she said, sounding shaken. "How did you know where it was?"

"Wasn't it here? What, you mean the locker? I was the first one there at lunch, and there it was, stuck in the door, so I

took it down. Only Chuck saw it. But I told him it wasn't you."
Still stung by the way she'd retracted her hand, he was talking
as he might to a wild creature he'd frightened, and it was only
when his own voice caught up with him and he heard that
note in it, almost a plea, and saw how her expression, instead
of softening, was closing up—only then did he start to understand. Still, it was slow coming to him, because it was so
difficult to imagine someone thinking the worst of him when
he was trying to help, trying to do her a good turn when she
couldn't even remember to meet him. It was so difficult, in
fact, that he didn't want to ask her about it for fear of merely
admitting the thought. But he had to say something, because
it was becoming clearer by the second that she wasn't going
to. "I see what you're thinking," he said. "You think I did this."
Again he waved the torn paper at her, and again she stepped
back. "What, do you think I broke into your house and tore a
page out of your magazine—that I gave you in the first
place—and stuck it up on your locker, just so I could take it
down and tell you? Because if that's what you think then
you're crazier than I am for trying to help you. You need help
all right—and I just hope there's someone as stupid as I am
around when you see it."

His anger had risen in him like a wind, and now it whisked
him out the door before he even thought to leave; so he was
somewhat surprised to find himself standing on the sidewalk,
with Alice at the door saying his name. "Little," she called
again, just as she'd called her cat. When he glanced back, she
said, "*I* didn't say anything." Then he walked away.

PART THREE

33

Melissa slipped into her father's office and sat down in his chair, where no one else had ever been known to sit, and tried to feel like him.

Worse than not knowing what to do was her suspicion that there wasn't anything to be done but wait, and now the idea that she had to be ready without knowing what she ought to be preparing for pressed her patience. Who could have anticipated Alice Reinhart? Certainly not her father. Could her brother? Could it actually have been part of his plan to inflate the orders with this unlikely publicity, so far more unsavory than the advertising and yet so wildly effective? Or had he merely capitalized on what might have been—and might still prove to be—their misfortune? That seemed improbable too, and it occurred to her that Frank hadn't explicitly claimed responsibility for anything that had happened, any of the boon that had come of the bad, and that, if nothing else, was to his credit. Maybe he was simply better at being ready for anything, in the way of her father and his father before him.

Just when the Alice Reinhart problem had begun to seem like a brief, unseemly episode, concluded once all the parties had been spoken to—respectively mollified, reprimanded, or informed—the regional papers had picked up the story. In the *Milwaukee Journal,* it was a full story; in the *Chicago Tribune,* a few column inches under the rubric "Midwest," a designation provincial enough to spare them any further exposure.

Or so she believed until the newsweeklies showed up almost two weeks later with Alice's troubles catalogued and elaborated under the headlines "Trouble Brewing" and "Gutenbier: How Guten?" One article reproduced the infamous poster, which prompted an unexpected spate of calls, most expressing outraged taste, others asking where a copy could be found. She'd never had reason to think about the power and reach of these publications, but now the reckoning was unavoidable. Just on the newsstands, they were generating orders for the new beer that far outstripped the brewery's capacity to produce it. It could be a ruinous success, and maybe there was some justice in that. Hurried and ahead of schedule because of the press of orders, they were sending out the first shipment, for which there would be no payment until the second round of orders came in, and thus no more money to pay off the debts that attended such a push. Even with Beeksma's money they could barely meet the payroll, inflated as that was, with almost everybody working overtime. Meanwhile, Frank was reminding her, with some impatience, that she was not, after all, a little old lady balancing her checkbook.

She'd given up trying to conjure her father, but suddenly, as if surrender were the key, she had a clear sense of him. She knew what he would do, in the unlikely event of his finding himself in such a situation, and she determined to fire the culprits. Let them sue.

She was just reaching for the telephone to summon Henry when it rang. Her hand, as if the sound repelled it, jerked away, but only for a fraction of a second, and then she answered with a cautious "Hello?"

"We thought you were in there." It was Frank's secretary, Joan, sounding a note of triumph. "Transferring Mike Drury from Miller."

With a click a new voice came on, somewhat supercilious, saying, "I see you're having a little trouble there."

"Trouble?" she said, and as she did looked up to find Frank standing in the doorway, as if he'd caught her measuring herself for their father's place. Meanwhile, Mike Drury was saying, "You haven't read *Newsweek*?"

"Oh, that," she said. "Nothing we can't handle."

"We could help you."

"You're too kind."

"We're willing to go up five dollars a share."

"With all this trouble, Mike? Seems ill-advised, wouldn't you say?"

"Not if there's an opening."

"There's not," Melissa said, "but thanks. Thanks again. I'll tell the other stockholders."

"No need."

"Oh no?"

"No, none. You'd find them well enough informed."

There was something peculiar about this, it took her a second to see. "Then why try me?" she said, positive he knew exactly what percentage of the stock she held, short of the controlling interest he was after.

His answer was only, "Why not?"

"Yes," her brother said, still standing in the doorway when she'd hung up, "why try you?"—not at all what she'd meant, that she was a weak link, as his tone implied.

" 'Why not,' and I quote," she said.

"Smelling blood."

"Hallucinating is more like it."

"I don't know. I was on my way to show you this when Beeksma called." He displayed an envelope but didn't budge from the doorway, and finally she had to get up and look, like a child or animal lured, approaching his upheld hand. As soon as she reached him he identified it, "A complaint," lowered it with one crisp move into her hand, said, "We're waiting in my office," executed a neat about-face, and started off.

"Beeksma?" she asked, trailing him.

He stopped. He hesitated, not yet turning as if not quite sure he'd heard her, then cast over his shoulder a curious look. "That's the blood they're smelling," he explained.

34

In his office were Joan, Curtis, and Helen, "Personnel," with an extra chair pulled in for Melissa. For an instant all were silent while she read the document, but then Helen said with soft impatience, "I thought this was resolved." No one answered, and she went on sotto voce, "Not that I would know. Not that anyone ever tells me anything I should know if I'm supposed to do my job." At this point Melissa interrupted, announcing, as she handed the complaint like a completed task to Curtis, "I've already decided to fire them."

The lawyer said, "Let's not be hasty." He waited till Melissa met his eye, and Frank noted in the pause, in his expression, a familiar fatherly indulgence. "This requires a formal response," he said, "so we'll have to investigate—for the sake of documentation—and if we find the complaint's legitimate, we'll let the perpetrators go, reprimand Henry, clarify our policy, put it all in writing, and hope they like our timely action. But not to worry. They're not there to put people out of business. Also, it might not hurt to compensate Ms. Reinhart for her trials."

"Compensate her?" Frank objected. "Isn't that opening the door to all kinds of—"

"It's already open. There's no saying they won't go ahead and sue."

"You think she's after money? I've talked to this woman and she doesn't strike me—My impression was, she wanted to be left alone."

"She filed a complaint."

"I still say—" Frank insisted but stopped, not willing to expose the depth of his impression of Alice Reinhart. The possibility that he'd been manipulated by her into precisely this position seemed too remote even to contemplate, but now that it arose, his clear image of her became suspect, what was soft revealing itself as simply blurry, and he was not so sure of himself. Melissa was saying, "Maybe we didn't do enough. But if we fire Hauser and Cole?"

And of course that was another problem for him. "They've both been here over ten years," he said. "I don't think—"

"What? Frank, they're just—" She broke off when Jennifer, her secretary, opened the door.

"You better listen to this," she said, the intrusion so odd and commanding that they all sat for a moment before getting up to see. She'd put her Walkman on Joan's desk, unplugging the earphones, fiddling with it until she concluded, "I guess you have to use these. I thought there was some way." And then she turned the volume up and all of them bent in, an ear turned to the drone of a woman's voice saying, "That may be a gray area. But what's been done to Alice Reinhart isn't. It's as clear as Title VII of the Civil Rights Act." What followed Frank couldn't quite make out, until the woman spoke abruptly: "That's the law, Tom. And if those ads don't create the climate for that sort of tortious behavior, then I don't know what does."

Another voice—Tom's, no doubt—began to talk about mayoral politics, and Jennifer, reading their faces, withdrew the earphones. "Sorry," she said. "I got here as fast as I could. She said the ads are a kind of harassment, or they condone it, a whole kind of cultural harassment."

If he hadn't been so irritated, Frank would have laughed at the proprietary pleasure Jennifer took in conveying this choice item. "That's vintage Lillian," Curtis said. "That sort of collateral pressure. She knows a bit about creating a climate."

"Lillian Roth?" He hadn't recognized the voice.

"I know her," Melissa said. "She wouldn't sue us."

"Lillian? She'd sue her mother if it served her purpose." Curtis worked his jaw a moment while he thought. "This isn't encouraging," he said. "If I know Lillian, she isn't after money. She's making a point. And that, ironically enough, could get far pricier than throwing some mad money at Alice Reinhart. I can handle the complaint, but you'd better start looking for a labor lawyer."

Frank watched Curtis and Melissa exchange another glance—something there—and recalled how the last time he'd seen Lillian Roth she'd been having drinks with Curtis. And now Curtis seemed suspiciously quick with his dire judgment of the situation, just as it was looking more manageable, clearer by the moment, Alice finally emerging from the muddle in familiar form. *She* had been manipulated. "Now, Curtis," Frank said—abruptly, it seemed, since everyone started. "Without Alice Reinhart, there's nothing to this, right? That's it?"

"What do you have in mind, Frank? The law being what it is."

"I just think it's worth looking into. On the chance this isn't really her idea. Meanwhile, what's the worst case here? Can they do anything about the ads, an injunction or something?"

He was as amused as he was annoyed by the lawyer's expression, the slow bemusement leavening with distaste. "I'll have to look into that," Curtis said. "But how wedded to this campaign are we?"

"We're certainly not going to let one confused employee and her self-righteous, self-aggrandizing attorney dictate our marketing policy."

"And I don't have to advise you, do I, to take care about approaching Alice Reinhart? You wouldn't want to do anything that Ms. Roth could misconstrue as intimidation."

Frank turned to Melissa, who was asking Curtis, "What about Hauser and Cole? There has to be something."

Helen said, "Here's what we'll do. Suspend them with pay while we look into this. It's not punitive, so they won't have any recourse. It's a pain, though, everybody working overtime and double shifts and all."

Melissa stood as if to go. "Hold on," Frank said, and the others, who'd risen at her cue, halted too. "Melissa," he specified. "I need a word. The rest of you can go."

Only Curtis didn't move. "Something I should hear?"

"Not necessarily."

"In that case." He sat down. "Just to be on the safe side," he explained.

There was nothing to do but go ahead, so he explained that Beeksma—unused to being demonized in *Time* or made the subject of public comment ranging from righteous indignation at Gutenbier's impropriety to ridicule over the company's susceptibility to righteous indignation, let alone legal action— was getting squeamish.

"Yes, and I'm sure he has no tobacco holdings," Curtis remarked. "My money says it's a ploy to get his hand in deeper."

Frank watched him well after he'd finished, as if to say: And? When nothing further was forthcoming, he said, "I'm inclined to take him at his word. And I don't see what choice we have."

"Call his bluff."

Melissa stepped in, trying to be conciliatory, and proposed they change the ads, perhaps to something along the quaint lines she'd mentioned some time ago. "Haven't they served their purpose anyway?" she said.

Why, he asked her, if the ads were serving their purpose, would she want to drop them?

"Because something else could serve us equally well and not get us embroiled in all this controversy."

"It's the controversy that's serving us, Mel."

"Not if Beeksma wants out."

"That's what I wanted to talk to you about," he said. "I

thought it might mollify him if we shifted officers—only nominally, but he'd be none the wiser. He'll just see evidence of our concern. And when the complaint goes away and everything calms down"—he waved his hand, *voilà*—"we'll seem to've solved the problem." Melissa was looking at him blankly, so he added, "It's just a matter of buying time."

"I'm a little confused," she confessed, and, watching her work through her qualms before committing them to speech, Frank did believe she was, but not in any way she recognized. She *said* she was confused because she thought it was disarming, but what her questions, framed at last, finally revealed was her conviction that all he wanted out of this was her position: If the change were merely nominal, why should Beeksma see more in it? And if advertising were the chief source of their trouble, how would a simple change of personnel appease Beeksma? And if their problem with Alice Reinhart was so sure to go away—and how, really, could it be?—what difference could their switching positions make? That was the switch he meant, wasn't it?

What was there to say? He turned to Curtis, seeking help. "I'm with Melissa," Curtis said. "I don't see what could come of it, other than disruption."

To press his point would be to confirm their suspicions, their oddly—or not so oddly—mutual suspicions. With an effort (could he never again talk to his sister alone?) he held off, returned to Curtis, asked him, wasn't he friends with Lillian Roth?

"Guilty. Though we're more collegial than friendly, in all accuracy."

"Maybe you could call her, colleague to colleague."

"I plan to."

"Oh, you do?"

"Unless, of course, you think I shouldn't?"

"Why not?"

35

How much more satisfying it might have been if Frank hadn't suggested it he couldn't say, but there it was. Lillian, surprising him a bit because it wasn't her way to spare anyone a healthy wait, agreed readily, he might even say eagerly, to see him. Until he found her—sitting solitary at a table in the crowded lunchtime Greenleaf, pale as ever, crisp as linen, sipping a glass of iced tea—he had no idea how humid he was, how wilted his clothes were, steamed between the day's heat and his own. "Just the weather to make everyone at Gutenbier happy and rich, isn't it?" she greeted him. "Ready to settle?"

He hadn't yet taken his seat. "Settle what?"

"Curtis, please don't waste my time. You didn't get me here to chat."

"But I did."

"Well, then." She began to fold her napkin.

"Come on, Lil," he said. "Let's say we're here for the same thing. We're not exactly enemies in this."

"We both want . . . justice?" she suggested dryly.

"Ultimately, we both want what's right for Alice Reinhart."

She put down her folded napkin, gave it a pat, sat back in her chair, and studied him with her customary skepticism. "That's where I think you're wrong," she said. "I think what's right for Alice Reinhart is a different world."

This nonplussed him for a moment. "A tall order," he

observed then. "And the courts are going to adjudicate this alternative reality?"

"You see, Curtis? We're not working along the same lines at all."

"OK, but let's say the lines, these lines, our lines, do intersect somewhere ahead, we know they do. A common good we're after—wouldn't you say? A safe and happy Alice in a healthy community? Neither of them possible without—"

"How are you defining 'healthy community'? And a 'safe and healthy Alice'? I can't even begin to imagine what that would look like to you. Or, to be perfectly fair, to Alice either. I think you're both subject to the same corporate fancy. You're just better compensated."

"And what makes you so wise, O sage?"

Lillian exhaled a silent laugh and looked past him with long-suffering patience, her lips pressed in a distant half-smile. "I'm not wise. I'm just worn out. I've done too many reprimands and damages and dollars. I'm sick and tired of trying to nickel and dime an attitude to death. I want to try the source."

"Which surely isn't Gutenbier."

"Why not?"

"How many times, if ever, has anyone come to you with a complaint against us? Or have you ever heard of one? Gutenbier is one of the most employee-friendly companies imaginable—as long as you still believe people ought to work for a living, of course. There's *that*, the work, a crushing burden, but—it's a funny thing—people want it anyway. People *want* to work for Gutenbier, and a lot of people in Rensselaer do—not just in the brewery, but the farmers who grow hops and barley and corn and rice, and the people in trucking and refrigeration, someone making bottles, tending bar, or working at a liquor store."

"And who next, the Joads?"

"My point is, the company does substantially more good than bad, if it *does* any bad, and I'd take some convincing. My point is, to go after Gutenbier is to attack the community you claim to want to improve."

Her head at a quizzical tilt, Lillian considered him for a long minute. "Do you really believe that, Curtis?" she said. "Or, to frame it in more congenial terms, do you actually buy it? You know you could make the same argument for crack operations in some neighborhoods in Milwaukee."

"I'd hardly—"

"Objection overruled, Curtis, you're not in court. And you're not in some abstract world of the people according to Henry Ford. What you're in is a world where women are second-class, where it's OK—not just OK but even advisable—to view them according to their sexual parts and functions. First and foremost, no matter what it is they're doing, they're the ass on some calendar or the cleavage on a beer commercial. Why shouldn't some clod at Gutenbier grab Alice Reinhart's breast, when everything around him tells him that's just what she's for? What's amazing is that anybody's capable of thinking any differently, when every TV show and movie, every magazine and every ad teaches the same lesson. And then there's beer, the magic elixir to make it all come true— because, let's face it, sometimes things just aren't as easy as advertised, but the right beer opens up that passage into manhood, where all these women with their legs perpetually spread can be found, and if not, if it's not the right beer, then enough of it'll make it seem that way anyway, so what does it matter? Isn't that what Gutenbier is selling, Curtis? Some kind of testosterone paradise? Well, wake up. We already live there. *That's* discrimination. That's what this is all about."

Fascinated, discomfited, Curtis was trying not to stare. There was some truth to what she said, but the extremeness of it made him doubt even the little he was inclined to accept. When he was certain she was finished, he said, "It's really a remarkable argument, coming from someone like Alice Reinhart."

"My, my, and I'd mistaken you for one of the enlightened few."

"Lillian, how is it different, the way you're using this woman?"

For once, she looked genuinely perplexed. "How is it anything *but* different?"

"I'm guessing she's more interested in making a living—and maintaining something of a life—than becoming this year's poster child for an idea. Of yours."

"Of *mine*, Curtis? Where have you been? What *Alice* is interested in, what Alice *wants*, is for this not to have happened. And short of turning back time . . . " With a lift of her eyebrows, Lillian signaled the irrelevance of considering any other options.

It was a point he had already reached, but, because of his belief in the world's ulterior logic that any reasonable person would eventually recognize, he couldn't easily accept an impasse, evidence that Lillian, seemingly the most rational of creatures, wasn't. And so, relying on that one sure thing, the elastic capacity of argument, he kept on talking while he searched for a polite way to extricate himself without revealing that he thought her wit had finally failed her.

36

When the knock sounded at her back door, Alice was glad she was wearing her uniform. Its dramatic power didn't work at home, but the uniform did give her a protected feeling. Carrying the paper she'd been reading, had been reading daily since her first appearance in it, she went through the kitchen.

It was Frank Johnson. Her hand with the paper in it dropped and she stepped aside for him, less satisfied with her apparel now (though it did show she was serious about work), wishing it were something nicer, and hoping it wouldn't make him think she'd been expecting him, even though, in a way, she had. All the time she'd talked to Lillian Roth, she'd kept coming back to him, and that was how she came to see that nothing else, not revenge or justice or money or attention, mattered half as much as what Frank Johnson thought, and if getting any of them meant taking away from him, then she wouldn't do it. That was her decision. She'd made it and she'd waited and she didn't hear a word from him, and it was only after a few weeks that she saw what she'd missed. He couldn't appreciate what she wasn't doing unless he knew about it, and he couldn't know about it if he kept away from her, the way he'd been keeping away ever since their one night. She didn't even have a way of letting him know she understood why he was everywhere before and then afterwards nowhere to be seen, how he could say he would help and then not say a thing. So she'd called Lillian Roth, who in the form of the complaint had given her the opportunity to get his attention without asking for it and, at the same time, to show him her good will—because she never would go through with it, she couldn't. She was trying to find the way and words to explain this when Frank said, "Alice, how are you?"

He said it as if she'd been sick, and she understood at once that, in view of the complaint, she shouldn't say, "Fine." But she'd only had a chance to think about it before he went ahead: "We received your complaint today. I told you you could come to me."

"I didn't want to come to you," she said. "I thought I'd . . . bothered you too much already."

"Bothered me." He said it softly, smiling an unhappy smile and looking around the kitchen as if he'd forgotten something. Then he seemed to remember her, to study her, a puzzle. "The truth is, Alice, this is a much bigger bother. I'm under some constraint here. Don't know quite how to proceed. Our lawyer gave me strict instructions not to intimidate you. Not even to *appear* to. And now you say you thought you'd *bothered* me."

"You told your lawyer?"

"Oh, those instructions were quite general, if that's what you mean. Your action engendered a meeting—that can't surprise you. It's actually lawyers that I wanted to talk about. This whole business—and I know I'm on dangerous ground here, so tell me if I'm out of line—was it your idea? I'm asking because it surprised me. It didn't seem like you. Admittedly, I don't know much about that, not enough to say what you're like, though I thought I did, until . . . this . . ."

He'd begun in difficulty, frowning it through, and now, overwhelmed, he concluded with a shrug. While she thought about the question, he must have become impatient, because before she could answer he went on, pressing but in the gentle way of a doctor palpating a break: "Because it seems more like someone else to me, more like Lillian Roth, who's got a few things of her own to work out. And I'd hate to see you taken advantage of. I'd hate to see you . . . used—unless that's your plan."

There was something endearing about his expression as he gave up again, so faltering and uncertain from someone who was hardly ever either. Someone whose whole point as a person was power and certainty. She knew what it was she saw in such men, when they were so different. There was always a good fit—where the weakness was she could slip in, fill in, become an essential part of the kind of human engine that made the world run.

For the first time since he'd arrived she had the luxury of molding her appearance to the moment, tipping her head for effect, knowing from so many photos just what that would be. "Do you think that's what she's doing," she said, "Lillian Roth?"—as if the prospect troubled and fascinated her as subtly as Frank Johnson's own complicated attraction did. Without stepping close, she rose up on the balls of her feet and stretched toward him slightly to tell him in confidence, "I don't have a plan."

Now he looked somewhat disturbed himself, and it occurred to her that all the maneuvers she'd perfected with Alex, all the nuances of gesture and expression so well understood and deployed by them both, were utterly unfamiliar to Frank Johnson. It occurred to her that, as long as she concealed it, she had the upper hand. This had a peculiar effect, conferring on the unpracticed Frank Johnson an aura of innocence, so that she found herself wanting to take care of him.

"You said you would help me," she explained, "and I'm not saying you wouldn't—but I didn't see you, and I didn't know what to do. And there was this lawyer, Lillian Roth. And she was so—"

"Impressive," he murmured.

"The way she put it, it was like doing something right, something good. It wasn't personal. And if I thought it was doing anything to you, I wouldn't've done it. I wouldn't want to make trouble for you. I . . ."

She paused, searching for a workable way of saying it, that what she wanted was the very opposite, and he pressed her softly, "What, Alice?"

She said, "I would want to *help* you."

In his stillness she thought she could read all kinds of emotion, all colliding to befuddle the man's face. "That's nice," he said finally, and managed a smile seasoned with regret or longing or something else, she couldn't tell. "That's nice of you. Especially in view of my dereliction."

Regret, she thought, that's what it was, and she tried to mirror his smile, lips pressed in a line. "So the other night," she said, "that was like an accident?"

"I meant not helping when I said I would."

"I know."

"An accident? No. Before it happened I might have said a mistake."

"And now?" They had at last arrived at a rhythm she knew, the talk that was a sort of circling, each step easing them a little closer while they kept the pretense of their distance going. The maneuver was easiest, no effort at all, when the topic was sex, and there was no telling where the talk broke off and the thing itself began. But any subject would do as long as the understanding was there, and sometimes she wondered why they had to talk at all, why they didn't just reach for each other when they came to an understanding, though one could see an understanding where the other didn't, or understand something completely different, and then you might have her marriage or something even worse.

Now, he said, he didn't know what to say, and she said that was all right, he didn't have to. Then for a second they stalled, looking at each other and casting about and coming back to look each other in the eye again until his gaze, on one of its excursions, came to rest on her uniform and he said, "Are you between shifts?"

"This?" She touched the collar. "I just like the way it feels—the way it feels against my skin. It's . . . cool, and . . ." With a ticklish shrug she left the rest to his imagination, which taxed his conversational powers. Silence ensued, and she was beginning to think she'd miscalculated or lost her appeal when he took one step closer, pinched the tab of her zipper between his thumb and forefinger, and, saying in that same soft way she thought of as her own, "So we do have time?" inched her uniform open.

Hot as it was, she wasn't wearing anything else, and now he was considering her exposed skin as if it presented a problem, one he was still parsing as he cupped his hands around her shoulders and with the slightest sober pressure shucked her uniform down her arms. She didn't move, didn't speak, regarded him a little warily, as if she were helpless, bound about the waist and wrists in the bunched-up fabric while he studied her and then, like a sculptor confirming a finish, touched her, first with the pads of his fingertips, then his palms, following the arc of her rib cage, sinking with her stomach, sweeping the curve of her sides, molding his hands briefly to her breasts, rounding her torso to trail his fingers down her spine until, in the hollow of her back, he snagged her uniform with his thumbs and tugged it past her hips. It pooled on the floor. His hands glided over her buttocks and continued down her legs, Frank lowering himself as he went along. Felt through his fingertips, seen through his eyes, her flesh thrilled, a squirm of pleasure that ran deep, but when she found herself looking down at him, Frank Johnson at her feet, the sensation dimmed and in one uneasy instant gave way to the thought that he was trying to make up for the last time, or maybe prove something. Thinking now instead of feeling anything, she caught his hand and raised it to her mouth and rolled his middle finger in her lips, sucked it slick and wet, then, spreading herself with her other hand, guided it in. Making the face they always wanted for the photographs, she started to hump his hand, but suddenly Frank pulled away.

He was looking around like someone trapped. "What?" she whispered. Then, stooping, he tried to pull up her uniform. "What?" She said it again, more insistently, but all he said was, "We can't do this.

"Not like this," he added as he wrestled with her sleeves and finally gave up. "Not now."

Only when he put his arm around her bare shoulders and kissed her, careful as a first date, did she see that it wasn't that he didn't want her.

37

What's pussy-whipped? The question met her at the door, before she'd even noticed Jesse stationed at his computer.

"Why?" she said. This elicited nothing but a shrug, not even the least glance, lately an amateurish straining toward blasé, so she told him, "It's a thing some people say when a woman's in charge. You know the saying 'sour grapes'?"

He grudgingly allowed he did.

"So aren't you going to tell *me* now? Who's pussy-whipped?"

Without moving his eyes from whatever he was working on, he mumbled, "The brewery," and darted his mouse and clicked.

"Who says?"

He shrugged. She was mulling over the risks and merits of demanding his complete attention when he asked, "Where's my father?"

It occurred to her that he'd known all along what "pussy-whipped" was. "In Colorado," she said. "You know that."

"I mean, why isn't he here?"

"Come here." She walked into the living room and sat down on the sofa, but he only followed as far as the door, where he stood and waited, hands hanging. "You know about having babies," she said. "I mean, making them. The thing is, the two things, having and making, they don't have to go together. And some people, like your father, might be up for the making part without thinking ahead to the having. It's not about *you*. It's general, a general thing, not that your father doesn't want to be here or didn't want you or anything like that. He didn't know you. The way I see it, I'm lucky. I have you."

"It was just sex," Jesse declared.

"It seemed like more at the time."

"Maybe if he knew me."

"Maybe . . . ? Did you ever think, you might be lucky?"

"Yeah, right." As quickly as his weary cynicism cut her, she tried to tell herself that he hadn't meant it that way, a judgment on her adequacy as a mother, and even so, he couldn't know. He turned to go but hung back with the weight of a last word. "I want to ask him," he said, "myself," and went. She could hear him climbing the stairs, walking to his room, closing the door.

Gutenbier was pussy-whipped. Was she the dominatrix, then? Alice? Lillian Roth? And how, even in the limited sort of public consciousness Jesse was subject to, could that be made to jibe with the commercials and the complaint of harassment, discrimination?

Jesse wanted to know where his father was—fatherless, grandfatherless boy—wanted someone to steel his incipient manhood against the pussy-whipping of the world. As if she were the nerve center of the house, the house a hulking, sprawling body, she could feel him in his room, sulking, flipping through the pages of one magazine, another, popping up to pace the room, flopping back down on the bed.

It took the doorbell to remind her that Curtis was coming over, a thought that, till a mere hour ago, had cleared her mind of almost everything else. She let him in, murmuring that Jesse was in some kind of mood, and Curtis suggested they go to his place instead. He could make dinner. When she hesitated, he said, "Jesse too, of course."

In response to her summons, Jesse called down a polite "No, thank you." Again she heard the door click.

He was on his bed just as she'd pictured him, plugged into his Walkman, from which a tinny drone escaped. He looked at her, a long way off, until she motioned to his earphones. She was about to tell him, as she usually did, to call his Uncle Frank at home or work in case of trouble, but, thinking better of it, instead told him to call Mrs. Plummer, a close neighbor and his erstwhile babysitter. She smoothed his hair back, patted a kiss onto his forehead. He endured it, watching her hand alight as if it were a flying insect.

What was it like to be eleven, twelve? She tried to remember, and wondered, was the feeling different for a boy? Curtis, consulted, said it would be hard to say, never having been a girl himself and having been a boy so long ago—and what was it Jesse was going through? Did she know? She told him everything she could. For a minute, when she'd finished, he continued silent, driving. "I guess I'm going to have to try and find Jim," she said, then added, "Jesse's dad."

Curtis angled a look at her. "Maybe I could help."

"How?"

"Do things with the two of you. Or maybe just the one of him. Manly things." He rolled the words in a brogue and made a roguish face.

"I know how you can help me," she said confidentially, leaning as close as she could, belted and divided from him by automotive design. "Now that you mention manly things."

He wrapped his hands around the steering wheel purpose-fully, humorously, as if on a mission, though he had, for all his mockery, picked up speed, she thought, and the devilish smile he assumed every time he glanced her way now was amusing but also a subtle reminder of what, once mentioned, had become her obligation. His hurry, the anxious checking under his polished composure, quickened her interest, started an answering rush to reassure him. She settled back, wrapped in the anticipation and through it, as if it were a filter, feeling how the leather seat cradled her, the luxury, then noticing on the dashboard the temperature in luminous blue letters, 82 outside, 68 in. Now she thought about Ayn Rand, how he'd helped her father entice her into reading *The Fountainhead*—for what? In her cotton dress, the smooth leather against her shoulders, her arms, her calves, with her hair braided behind her, she all at once felt like a child, that curious, gawking girl again, being taken for a ride, and, like a girl, she took a sidelong peek at Curtis. He could have been in another world, for all he knew about the temperamental shift. When he turned and smiled this time, it made him just as suddenly seem pitiable, and in a burst of sympathy, she squeezed his hand. "I'm serious," he said. "About Jesse? His father could complicate things considerably."

"You mean about money?"

"Among other things. He's a wealthy eleven-year-old. It has to be thought about."

"I don't see why. It's not like he's spoiled. And if you mean Jim—"

"You're right," he said before she could finish. "Why worry before you have to? *If* you have to. If anyone has to. Worry. It's hardly necessary, now that I think about it." He went on then, reflecting on worry, the emotion, the activity—was there any purpose to it?—sounding like her father when he thought aloud, except without the testing edge to every question, as if he knew not just the answer but what she would say, though that might have been a tender daughter's impression and not her father's fault at all, if it even was a fault, to seem to know everything she wanted to know.

In her infatuated teenage years she'd known as if by intuition where Curtis Niemand lived, so she wasn't surprised when he pulled up to the two-story brick building whose second floor he occupied, although, because so much time had passed since she'd made a study of the place, it did seem different in a curious way, starker, sharper, somehow more real. The inside, which she'd never seen but had imagined in detail, was something else entirely.

They'd just come in when Curtis excused himself to make a culinary investigation, stopping midway to the kitchen to retrace the few steps to his stereo and ask her, would she like to hear something? There was a record (vinyl!) already on the turntable, and she told him whatever was on was fine. At once the first round notes of a trumpet filled the room, announcing a Haydn horn concerto she'd heard often enough at her father's to know it by heart.

Left alone to look around, now she noted the particulars of what she'd felt on walking in, how rich the room was, lavish in its subtle way—the gleaming floor, the Persian rug, the elaborate molding of a satiny red wood, the wall of books behind glass, the leather couch and high white walls rosy in the late sunlight, even the generous view of wooded hills unfolding from a field, a hazy swath of green swept here and there with the pink and yellow, lavender and white of drifts of wildflowers. It was all so extravagant compared with what she'd once envisioned. He'd moved here at the time of his divorce, a circumstance that had worked its way into the setting she'd conjured up for him, shadowy backdrop for so many daydreams. Because he'd seemed so unhappy then, a man in need of care and comfort, his home had taken on a dark and meager aspect in her imagination, which, itself furnished at the time by *Crime and Punishment, Jane Eyre, David Copperfield*, and *Sister Carrie*, supplied Curtis Niemand with narrow hallways, brittle shades pulled halfway down, sparse castoff furniture, threadbare rugs, and tubercular neighbors, none of whom were young or pretty. The interior picture composed of nothing but his pallor and her paltry stock of romantic images nonetheless remained strong enough to render the reality utterly alien—all so different and comfortable that for one disoriented instant she was completely bemused—almost offended—by how easy he'd actually had it after all.

But when she wandered to the kitchen and watched him undetected as he considered the contents of one cupboard, then another, he once again became that sad and solitary being, living alone in an apartment. In the light of her presumption, suddenly revealed for the harsh thing it was, the sight of him stirred up a confusion of tender feelings. As if it were a sound, he turned and raised his eyebrows—What?—and when she didn't answer, asked her, "How's your appetite?"

She smiled, and in the second she took to see how he'd meant the question he saw how she'd taken it, how she'd meant her smile, and crossed the room, head held at a thoughtful tilt, much as he'd looked deliberating over his menu. He kissed her in the doorway, then again in the dining room, and in the living room he sank onto the sofa, pulling her around to face him. Holding his shoulders to steady herself, she lodged on his lap. He was looking at her skirt where it had ridden up when she'd spread her legs to sit astride him, and now he slipped his hands up around her hips and lifted the dress. "This," he said, gazing at her body as he uncovered it, "is a fine fashion." His hand tightened on her and, his voice tightening too, he said, "If you could make a small adjustment." She raised herself and helped him unfasten his pants, awkward. His fingers were at her crotch, pulling aside the elastic, working at her, so that when she let herself down again she slid right onto him. He made a soft sound, half contentment, half impatience, and she began to move.

His zipper bit her thigh. She moved, tried to avoid the pinch without losing her rhythm. Curtis, sensing something, shifted, worked his fingers in between them, searching, massaging while she rose and lowered herself, and then his fingertip slipped to one side but kept up its motion against the slippery flesh until in a paroxysm of clumsiness his hand fumbled and fell aside and he groaned, gathered himself up, slumped abruptly like a puppet dropped.

She could still feel the throbbing inside, his subsiding, hers grasping, less and less, then letting go. Her eyes wandered from his serene face, fell upon the table next to them, beyond the hump of the sofa's arm. There was, like a peculiar museum exhibition, *Captain Sir Richard Francis Burton*, just as she'd found it in her father's study, open facedown with glasses perched across its spine—Curtis's glasses, it took her a second to see. He had started stroking her sides. She looked up past him at the wall, the glassed-in shelves of books, curious. Almost at once she spotted *Tent Life in Siberia* by George Kennan, nearby T. E. Lawrence's *Seven Pillars of Wisdom*, in fact a full section of desert adventure much like her father's. Then there was polar exploration, *Endurance*, *Shackleton*, even the book she'd bought her father, so hard to find, Shackleton's own book *South*. There were the Tuchmans and the Shirers, a whole shelf on World War II, another on the Civil War, the rise and fall of this and that, the Third Republic, the great powers, the Third Reich, the Roman Empire. So many books, the same ones in her father's library—they'd always given her a sense of the vastness of what she didn't know, at once intimidating and inspiring, because it was her father's and therefore wise beyond her years and grasp but, also because it was his, within her reach, hers for the asking once she learned how.

Now, though, the feeling was claustrophobic, the two men, walled in by books, poring over their war stories like a couple of schoolboys who'd never even known a scrape. When she concentrated her gaze on the Russian novels, the picture became even more ludicrous, of the mutual ravishing of Natasha, lovely Natalia, spilling from the open page onto their quiescent, impressionable laps. And then, unbidden, unexpected, the vision of her father heaving himself onto Annie, mounting Sue, supplanted the ridiculous Russian fiction, erased all the rest, even the books right before her, a blur now that she tried to read more of the titles. She found herself staring down at Curtis, who was watching her as well, with a sated drowsy look, the contented flesh softening along his square jawline. "What about you?" he said, soliciting her wishes with a smile like Santa Claus.

"Me? I'm fine."

"I could've told you that, but what—"

"Weren't you making dinner when I interrupted you?"

He laughed, plopped out of her, puddling. "All that and dinner too?" he said, shifting as she maneuvered her knee around so she could climb off without soiling the sofa, alarmed now that they hadn't used a condom, that she hadn't even thought of it, that everything was suddenly flesh and fluids, practical and concrete, the stuff, when, only—what was it? five minutes ago?—close to the height of physical pleasure, just short of the body's apogee, there had been no body to it at all, no skin or limbs, no hair or holes or wet, only desire, a phantasm of the overburdened senses.

38

With more deliberation than he usually put into having a beer, Little had chosen to sit at a table in the dark corner of Losers, far enough from the door that anybody who could just stop at a stool probably wouldn't make the added effort to obtain his company. But Cole and Hauser, with more time on their hands now, made the trek, and so once again he found himself sharing a table with them. If he'd imagined that his mild intercession on Alice's part would put them off, he was wrong about that too, because, with a sympathetic reception virtually assured them at Jonah's or Fish Feathers, Cole and Hauser had come to Losers expressly to find him. He'd been in the lounge when they were called out and was still there when they returned and, huffy with injustice, comparing looks, jerked their belongings out of their lockers, grabbed their lunches, and walked out. Someone had asked where they were going, earning a last cold look from Hauser as he left the room, but Cole had answered with a grimace, "To look for a lawyer." "What, his wife finally reported him?" someone muttered when Cole was well out of range, and a few of the men chuckled, but nothing else was said.

So Little didn't know the truth of what he'd heard in the talk and speculation that went on after that, but he was as good as positive that the two of them had been fired, and that it had to do with the Alice business, happening too soon after the story went around to be anything else. Alice was working tonight, still subjected by scheduling to Cole and Hauser even now that they wouldn't be there, but he suspected that she'd be especially pleased with the extra work now that her shift was down to two men. Busyness seemed like a drug to her, though one she couldn't administer to herself—which was how he made sense of his onetime luck with her: In the empty hours he was something to do.

As soon as Hauser opened his mouth, Little guessed they'd been to their usual haunts after all, were putting in at every port on St. Anne to spread their story of woe. "Your girlfriend," he said, or broadcast, with the amplitude and flourish of a proclamation.

"Who?" Little asked.

"Who?" Hauser echoed it derisively. "The one that screwed up my life, is all. The one who comes in and starts messing around with something worked for hundreds of years—"

"Hundreds?" Little inquired mildly.

"Fuck you. Oops. I hope I didn't offend you. Don't tell Alice. I don't want to get a detention."

"Show him the pictures," Cole cut in, and Hauser snapped at him, "I'm gettin' to that." When he said this, he raised his hand in an abortive swat, and Little noticed that he was holding a roll of paper. "Your girlfriend." He wagged it under Little's nose, then sat back as if to watch the effect of his devastating argument.

Little regarded him curiously, ventured another "Who?"

"Good question. You think someone who poses for pictures like this can complain about a *cal*endar? That *nobody* ever *noticed* before?" He was trying to unfurl his roll with a flick, but the papers only loosened, maintaining their curl. Finally, he flattened a hand on each of the opposing corners, obscuring the familiar turned face of the girl on all fours. Noticing, he hinged up his hand to reveal the face like young Alice's. "She's the one who should be out on her *ass*. Which I guess she would like, from the look of it. Fuckin' *hypocrite*." This last word he seemed to expel, a stinging mouthful of acid, as if it were the ultimate indictment. Almost at the same time he saw that the pictures, which he now tried to fan out, were not prompting any reaction from Little, who merely glanced at the pages, by now so handled and wrinkled and smeared that they resembled his own soft-focus memories of the Alice he'd once imagined. "Oh, I get it," Hauser said, his intuitive cunning dulled to a slur, "that's how you *like* it. Who cares if the cunt is a bitchy priss of a bitch to people like us when she's a"—he sputtered—"Penthouse—Puppy!—at home. Who cares what she does to someone else's *life* if she sits on *your* face."

Calmly Little told him, "You don't get anything. You don't get anything, because you're a prick, and getting nothing is what you deserve. Alice Reinhart isn't my girlfriend. And this girl isn't Alice Reinhart. The only reason she has the pictures is because I gave the magazine to her back then, when I thought they *were* her. That's how I know. And that's how I know you broke into her house—because I know where you got these." He started to reach for the pages, but Cole's hand, surprisingly quick, darted out and grabbed them, one crumpled bunch.

Instead of looking the least bit surprised, Hauser laughed, one rough loud throat-clearing exclamation. "Well, you think you know everything, don't you, Mister—" He broke off, apparently unable to think of an adequate epithet, and Little had to suppress a laugh, unwise as it would've been. "When the truth is, you don't know shit. First, this is her." He pointed vehemently at the empty table where the pages had been. "Anybody could see that. Except if somebody's leading you around by your dick. Second, it's not like we went off on *Alice*." He spoke the name like a taunt. "It just so happens we're under in*struc*tions from a higher power."

"Getting fired?" Little said. "That was part of the grand plan?"

"Fired?" With elaborate wonder Hauser swiveled slowly to

ask Cole. "Does he mean our paid vacation? That's right, Little big man, *paid*."

Somewhat shocked—but maybe this was just a stage, he thought, the way such proceedings went—Little sat there, stolid, as the two stood up, Hauser first, saying to Cole, "Let's go. It stinks in here."

He was still sitting there sometime later, reviewing the exchange and trying unsuccessfully to come up with a clever response to Hauser's parting line, when Rick came in, picked up two beers at the bar, and brought them over. "Buy you one?" he said, setting a bottle before Little, and sat down. He should've known better, he said, had made the mistake of stopping at Jonah's, where Cole and Hauser were now holding forth. News that Little had just been subjected to the same performance silenced him for a few seconds, while he seemed to reflect on their mutual rotten luck. It was then that he remarked, "I woulda sworn they got canned."

"I thought they were hosin' me."

"What?"

"When they said they were still getting paid."

"You think they'd work for free?" Rick's mock incredulity faded as the two of them regarded each other with the growing suspicion that they were talking their way around some misunderstanding.

"OK," Little said. "They're out. I know that. What I didn't buy, which they said, was they got paid leave."

Rick shrugged, contented with the mystery of it. "They said they were goin' to work. When I saw them. Just left, like when I did." Then he offered, as if in explanation, "Late shift."

Little looked at the clock, barely visible in the dim clutter behind the bar, and with an effort made out that it was after seven. "Shit," he said. "Are you sure?"

With a shrug Rick conceded that "sure" was a flexible term for him. Though Little had gotten up, he didn't really know what to do next. What if he rushed off to protect Alice only to find her undisturbed, except by himself? The impulse to help wasn't personal anymore, would've applied to anyone, not just Alice, but that didn't make the chance of looking like a fool any easier. But, then, if he was really acting on general good will, how could it matter what Alice thought?

Adding to Rick's impassive perplexity, he left abruptly, with little more than a nod, in his preoccupation fixing on one measure at the very least: He ducked back into Losers and borrowed first a phone book, then some change from Sunny, then leaned in the doorway next to the pay phone, flipping through the book for Melissa Johnson's number. She was listed—it seemed a reassuring sign of her concern. But when he dialed the boy answered, said she wasn't there, and again Little didn't know what to do. "All right," he said, "no message, thanks," hung up, and stood there for a second staring at the telephone as if it were the only thing that held him steady while the moment, gathering force, became so strong he felt its pressure through his back, his legs, his neck. He called again. This time a man answered, said, "This is her brother, Frank. Maybe I can help?"

"I don't know," Little said. "It's about— Can you tell her—" *What?* "It's just a little problem at the plant, I guess I can handle it, but you tell her I called—Joe Martin, they call me Little."

"What kind of problem?"

"Nothing major, no problem, not really, she'll know, but thanks," and before Frank could ask anything else, Little hung up. Already he was beginning to feel ridiculous, the risk to Alice seeming less and less real by the moment, maybe even a sign that he wasn't really so indifferent to her after all. But he hurried himself along anyway and reached the plant just as the light was fading, which suited him—if only it were as dim inside when he encountered Steve, and then Walt, whose surprise at his presence compelled him to lie, claim to have been called in at the last minute because of a scheduling glitch.

From Walt this elicited exactly the information he was after. "Must be some glitch," he said, elaborating, naturally enough, that Hauser and Cole, also not scheduled, had shown up too.

"Yeah?" said Little, as if this were an intriguing coincidence. And where were they now? Walt didn't know, and when Little opened his mouth to ask where Alice was working he couldn't produce the question. So instead he wandered around—the huge chamber that housed the mash kettle and lauter tun, through the wort-chiller room, the storerooms, even the lounge, where, since nobody was there, he paused to knock on the bathroom door. It was a relief that Cole and Hauser were nowhere to be found, though this would have been far more comforting if Alice herself were anywhere in evidence.

It wasn't entirely unlikely that on a short shift with so little supervision they'd have a worker as new as Alice doing maintenance, so he proceeded to the cavernous fermenting cellar, which was utterly deserted, then on to the cool vault where aging tanks stood in their monumental ranks. On the threshold he stood still and listened, hearing nothing at first. Then one of the tanks made a distinct noise, and he noticed the stepladder and, instantaneously, a shoe and a blue cuff coming out the manhole on the side. The delicacy of the small foot in its sneaker seeking the uppermost rung of the ladder identified it as Alice's. In his relief Little found her dainty blind foot, feeling its way through the air like a mole, peculiarly touching. As he took a step forward Alice found her footing, backed a few steps down the ladder, and then tilted over the edge of the hole, back into the tank, the soles of her feet lifted clear of the rung. She emerged with her pail and brushes in her hand.

Surprising him somewhat, because he wasn't aware of making any noise himself, Alice looked straight at him, smiling, although as soon as she saw him her smile disappeared. She wasn't just not smiling at him—she was frowning, actually looked alarmed. He remembered that she thought he'd bur-gled her house. His first impulse was to back up, lift his hands, show he wasn't a threat—an undertaking so unfair it stopped him at once. That was when he heard something behind him, a shuffling with some weight to it, turned, and took a chop across the head and the neck, so sharp that his knees buckled, but he was still turning as something struck his head one more time.

39

What she understood the second she saw them she instantly thought she'd known all along—because hadn't she told the paper?—that Hauser and Cole had done it. Hadn't she known, down underneath her relief at finding the photos still there, that something had stopped it, the search through her things, something satisfying enough, as the magazine had once been for Little, and hadn't she seen that? And as she understood it she felt him fall, a plummeting echo in her own heart. At the bottom was panic. They were drunk— she could tell from the way they were walking, even the way Cole cocked his arm, wielding a Gutenbier bottle so clumsily that its weight more than Cole's swing seemed to hit Little. But, drunk as they were, she was amazed at how fast they got from the doorway to the foot of her ladder. Little wasn't moving. Hauser held on, one hand on either side of her, as if he were steadying the ladder or, once he leaned into it, wavering himself. "Happy now?" he said. "Now that you got your way? We know who you are, and just because nobody else does, when they do you'll see what who . . ." His jaw hung slack for a second, and his eyes wandered as if in pursuit of his point. He had the magazine or some of its pages, she saw, flattened under his hand where it was gripping the ladder, and she wondered how fast that hand could move if she jumped over the side. She could kick him away, but she was the one in the unsteady place, Hauser flat on his feet. She could scream. She opened her mouth, but nothing came out. She was wondering, what if he was like an animal that became more dangerous when you upset it and then no one heard her, or what if he wasn't dangerous now, only drunk and mad, and a scream turned him vicious?

"I need to get down," she said to Hauser, who sneered as if it were something ridiculous. Her voice had gone furry and strange. Hauser slanted a look back at Cole, then in a husky mimicry of her said, "I need to show you something." To loosen his hand without losing the pages proved difficult for him, a crablike maneuver of the fingers that then turned the gathered paper over and opened to the picture of her on her knees with her head on her arms and her rear in the air, her underpants around her feet. Though she barely looked, only enough to see what it was, the underpants made an impression, as they hadn't all the times she'd studied the picture, cotton briefs with blue flowers and sewed-on elastic, childish and cheap. It made her teary, but not the picture—the fright, and the idea of being seventeen and wishing that something would happen.

Hauser had presented the pages like evidence, with a jerk of his hand and his jaw, but now he was gazing at the picture himself, slack in the face again. He took an audible breath. "You fuckin' cunt," he said in his throat, raising his red eyes, and she jumped—but he grabbed her, got her by her arm, twisted in a grip that she only noticed when she could breathe again, since the thrust of her launch had knocked her wind out. What she saw then was his hand where it had darted out and gotten her, so fast that some of the pages had come along and were pressed on her now, under his hold, like something to keep his hand clean. She'd gotten her breath back enough to see this, and she screamed. First there was a catch, then a sound that stopped her, frightening as it was, and so strange coming out of herself that for an instant she didn't believe it. Then the sound rose up again, howling like something dying. Hauser clapped his hand over her mouth. She choked on the sound. He hoisted her up like a sack on his arm and shoved her back into the manhole, halfway, so she was jackknifed over the opening. It was cutting her stomach. She fumbled for the stepladder with her foot.

When he'd pushed her he'd dropped his hand, so she screamed again, startled at the sound echoing all around like something pursuing her from every side. Outside she could hear a mutter or a laugh—low and garbled, as if it were far away, down a tunnel. "Go ahead," Hauser said from her side, where he'd squeezed his head against her in the opening. "Go ahead, scream." She threw her weight against him and his voice wrenched off. For a second, a minute, however much time she couldn't tell, there was silence. She tried kicking Hauser, kicking up and out like a donkey, but struck only air, brushed something with her shoe, the knob on her ankle, her knee, and then Hauser bore down on her, wrapped his arms around her legs above the knees, if it was Hauser, except she heard him at the same time as if from far away saying, "Do that. Do like that."

With a squeeze of the arms on her legs Cole's voice, closer, behind her, grunted, "You."

She said, "What?" She cried it, another scream, just the piercing beginning with its ripples scraping her ears. Again that laugh, a rumble at her back, and Cole, with a shove for emphasis that pinched the trapped flesh on her belly, said, "The doggy one."

He repeated it—at least it sounded like, she couldn't hear, didn't want to, was trying to think herself free, a thought coming up from her body, simple and pure as a message to move or eat or sleep.

There was more muttering, shuffling she wasn't sure she heard until it ended up at her, a rough touch instead of a sound, a hand, then another one grabbing her uniform, a scrabbling, a fistful of cloth at her hip. An arm lifted her up like a doll, slid right up where she hung over the edge of the manhole, and caught at her collar, her zipper, and jerked. The hands on her were as fast as they were clumsy, faster, like frantic things, with every fumbling, until they were nothing but force, ripping the zipper off the fabric, yanking the cloth, then, when it wouldn't give, the collar, so that her head was hauled back. She was choked faint for the minute it took him to strip the uniform over her shoulders, twisting her arms behind her to do it. When the spell passed, she felt around, flailed, but someone shoved her headlong back into the hole. It was cold metal now against her raw skin, digging into her so hard she thought she was going to vomit, so she tried pushing up on her toes to ease the pressure—but just as she did, one of them yanked her uniform over her feet.

They were grabbing her legs now, prodding her knees. It felt like a hundred hands on her. She tried to twitch away and they fastened on, tightened, one crushing her bent leg against the tank. All she could do now was squirm, and that made them laugh again, that laugh again, with the shuffling, scuffling sounds and the ladder shuddering under her. If she squeezed to one side, if she pressed her sweaty palm hard on the slick inside of the tank and propped herself up, she could see behind her. Hauser was at her back, fishing his penis out of his pants. Seeing her looking, he was inspired to cram his fingers into her crotch and hold them up for her, dripping. Feeling her leg free, she kicked again, and Hauser yowled and then in another voice yelled, "You stupid fuck," and her leg was pinioned again just as Hauser threw his weight against her, shoving with his penis and missing and missing and hitting her bone. He was flopping and slipping, only half hard, bending up against her like rubber.

Shaking, dripping from the eyes and the nose and with bile in her mouth from being hinged on her gut, what she felt on realizing Hauser's condition was relief, a pang indistinguishable from panic in her chaotic state. "Bitch crippled me," he wailed, the same cry of outrage as when she'd kicked him.

Then she cried out too, heard it before she knew it, because she was focused, all her senses like a fist, on her crotch, the crushing pain where something had rammed her. It hit her again and she thought her bones were crumbling. It was a bottle, the bottle he'd been holding. Through her pain she could even feel the beaded rim on the bottom as Hauser battered her with it, tried screwing it into her weeping hole. She was moving as much as she could—one way, then the other—trying to elude it and crying, not caring about the crushing chorus of echoes. It was different then—she couldn't feel anymore, the pain like a medium she was suspended in, spreading every sensation in every direction so there were no distinctions, just one quivering mass—but then it was different, parted with a throb and poured into her as if all the pain battering to get in had finally pierced her, and she cried with relief. It was the neck of the bottle. She could feel the mouth, the lips, each time he shoved it into her.

And then there was nothing—a second of stillness—and she thought she'd died, till the throbbing began again and at the same time the air all around her percussed as if shaken by an explosion. The ladder flew out from under her feet. She hung on to the tank inside, or tried, but her hands slipped on the glass. Limp as she'd felt for that instant, like a doll dropped, suddenly an astonishing wave of energy lifted her, literally lifted her—she arced through the air, then saw that it was Little, who plucked her from the manhole, set her on her feet. That was all he had time for, not even a look, because Cole and Hauser—one on either side of him, where they'd fallen—were picking themselves up. In the same motion, they were on Little, who staggered, trying to shake them off. Alice hurled herself at the three of them, thinking to help him, but she glanced off Cole's back like a bug flicked aside.

On wobbly legs, hunched over her cramped stomach like a monkey, she ran screaming past the aging tanks, through the fermenting cellar, up to where, over the roaring of the wort into the lauter tun, she could hardly hear herself. The one named Steve was up at the controls. One she didn't know was below, coming around the mash kettle from the direction of the lounge. She screamed at them, explaining, pointing, begging them to hurry, and then, when, for all her frantic efforts, the two of them stood there and stared at her, as if she were a monkey with the power of speech, she just screamed and screamed, not even trying to make sense.

40

She'd just turned to wave as Curtis drove off, when the door opened behind her and she turned to find herself face to face with her brother, stern as the revelation he was. Her alarm must have been evident, because he said without softening, "Something frightened Jesse."

"Something?" Then, as Frank was explaining—nothing, actually, a sound or a spooky thought—she caught sight of Jesse on the stairs, attentive until he saw her looking, at which point his eyes scuttled to find another focus. "Mrs. Plummer wasn't home?"

The instant it occurred to her to wonder at her brother still blocking the door, he eased around her, easing her around. "We got a call," he was telling her, "about some kind of trouble at the brewery."

"What kind?" Now she was trailing him, almost bumping into him when he stopped abruptly, apparently to think, before replying that he didn't know. "Someone called Little. He said you'd know." He glanced back to observe her reaction—which was to hurry past him, perturbed. If there was trouble, why weren't they going? And had he called the police? This stopped him at the car as he stepped around to the passenger side. "He didn't say it was anything like that," he told Melissa, a peculiar note of protest in his voice.

The brewery looked especially calm, the familiar old glass globes casting a mellow glow across the bricks at regular intervals. Inside, though, a strange sound greeted them, unrecognizable through the churning of the plant that roared, over-whelming everything as they approached the mash kettle.

For one stricken second Melissa tried to apprehend what she was seeing, and then she ran forward, not knowing what she meant to do. It was Alice Reinhart, naked, her arms wrapped around her waist, and she was screaming—scream-ing at two other dumbstruck employees, whose eyes lighted on Melissa and Frank as they came in. Alice turned and Melissa saw that she was bleeding, or had been bleeding, stains smearing the insides of the thighs to her knees, her pubic hair matted rusty red. As they moved toward her she kept screaming, staring befuddled behind her open mouth, like a baby stuck in a shriek. Melissa reached for her, too shocked by the look of her to think yet what to do, but Alice fell into Frank's arms. So unexpected, this startled Melissa into a practical turn: Where was the villain? Where was Joe Martin? The police should be called. An ambulance. They had to get Alice to a doctor.

Alice had stopped screaming now, was shuddering against Frank's chest with a gulping sob, and Melissa, touching a ten-tative hand to her shoulder, had started to ask "Who—" when a man came staggering, drunk or hurt, out of the hall that led to the fermenting cellar. It was one of the two they'd dis-missed today, Cole, and, unsteady as he was, he was running, lurching this way and that like a blind rat in a maze. He caught sight of Melissa and charged at her, proclaiming like an indict-ment, "You!"

Melissa dropped back a step and saw that Frank, now abreast of her, had moved Alice aside—needlessly, because Cole stopped short and, like one restrained by an invisible fence, railed at Melissa just out of arm's reach. Mostly he was incoherent—or at least she couldn't understand him—but he seemed, with an unmistakable tone of vindication, to be berat-ing her for the decline of Gutenbier. "Your fuckin' policy," was the only clear refrain. He said she didn't know what she was doing, besides wrecking everything, and, "We were doing great until you came along!" He said that her father never would've fired him, never would've fired any hardworkin' stiff for a slut like that, and her brother wouldn't've either, wouldjou, Frank? At this peculiar note of intimacy, Melissa looked curiously at her brother, who lunged for the man, but not before he could say triumphantly, "But not for long, right, Frank? Right, Frank, we're gonna—"

Frank, though considerably slighter than Cole, knocked the man down with ease and knelt on him, an improvised hold, his hands timid, wandering, before they struck. Cole looked up at him slack-faced and blinked. "What the hell," he said, "didnjou say . . . ," and then, when Frank didn't respond, except to cede his grip to the other two employees who'd run to help, Cole erupted in a fury that shook off the surprised men for an instant. "We had a deal!" he was bellowing. "We had a deal!"

Melissa stared at his contorted face, then at Alice, who was staring too, who, when Frank returned to her side, shrank from him. He was taking off his shirt to put it around her, and she managed to pluck it from him, to cover herself, without having him touch her. Melissa stepped over. "Frank," she said, "why don't you get something out of the locker room? Or a uniform out of the lounge? Steve? It's Steve, right? Go call the police. And an ambulance—Alice, an ambulance? Or would you rather I took you to the hospital?" Alice nodded, and Melissa, interpreting, told Steve to forget the ambulance. "It's not him," Alice whispered. Melissa bent to her. "Not just him," she said.

"That other one?" Melissa asked. "Hauser? Where is he? And Joe—Little?"

Alice was staring at the doorway Cole had come through. Turning, Melissa sickened to see the man emerge, blood running from his nose and mouth, one eye squeezed in a swelling mass of purple flesh, his narrow body angled forward, trudging headlong with the inexorable gait of an automaton, gripping in his hand one of their bottles, broken and bloody. Only when this last gory detail registered did Melissa come awake to the situation. "Get Frank and Steve," she said to Alice, nudging her in their direction, but the woman wouldn't move. "Go!" Melissa shouted, starting at the sound she made, although it made no impression on Alice, who merely stared at the oncoming Hauser with a wildly vicious look, as if with her rage and loathing alone she expected to topple the man.

Melissa looked around for a weapon. There was nothing nearby. Alice was stuck to her side, so that, when she spotted a mop propped in a bucket against the wall and started toward it, they stumbled together like a collapse in a three-legged race. From this confusion, Melissa looked up to see Frank flying at Hauser—an act of athleticism and bravado that, once she'd breathed a moment of pure relief, astonished her. It seemed to astonish Hauser too: With time enough to defend himself, he only gaped and went down grunting. And here were the police, in all the commotion, two officers picking Frank off Hauser. Melissa couldn't think clearly, even enough to steer Alice toward the clothes Frank had brought in before he'd leapt at Hauser. Alice was the one who moved—and toward Hauser, until Melissa pulled her away.

"There's another one," Melissa said to the policeman who was asking for information. "I mean, someone else, not like these. Maybe hurt," she persisted, just as a second pair of policemen arrived and conferred with the first two, then with Melissa and Alice, asking where they thought the other perpetrator might be. "Victim," Melissa corrected them.

The police, once they'd handcuffed Hauser and Cole, tried to get someone to tell them exactly what had happened, focusing on Alice, who was brushing them off like pests while Melissa insisted they leave her alone till she'd been to a doctor. In the midst of this, the paramedics who'd appeared with the second pair of policemen came down the hall bearing Little on a stretcher. Alice ran along after them, gazing down as if trying to recognize the familiar figure there and, only when the medics had reached the door on the other side, tenderly touched his battered face.

"Now, *his* name—" one of the officers was saying to Melissa, his notebook flipped open and pencil poised.

"He's alive," Alice reported in a murmur, and Melissa took hold of her arm and led her away, fending off the police with assurances that Alice would talk to them as soon as she'd been to the hospital—and meanwhile surely someone else—perhaps Frank—could answer their questions. As the one policeman followed them, pressing, she heard her own voice rising with impatience. The tone disappeared when Alice, whispering in an effort not to interrupt, asked if she could lie down in back instead of sitting in the passenger seat.

At the hospital, at Alice's murmured request, she stood by through as much as she could stomach of the exam—the palpating and swabbing and taking of samples while a lab technician took photographs and a counselor hovered explaining—until finally, on the pretext of going to the bathroom, she stepped between the curtains and sat down in the hall. This was where she was when a hand touched her shoulder and with a start she looked up and found Sue. "Go away," she said, and dropped her forehead into her hand.

"I'm not working," Sue said quickly. "I was—when I heard—it *is* my beat—but I thought you might need someone. Frank told me I'd probably find you here."

"Did he? Isn't that ironic."

"I don't know. That'd be a first for Frank."

"Could my brother be evil?"

Melissa rolled her forehead on her hand to angle a look up at Sue, who blinked like somebody just splashed, then said, "It depends."

"On what?"

"What did he do?"

"That's the question."

Sue gave this some thought. "Then I guess it depends on

what you call evil. Because I don't think Frank would do any-thing *he* would call evil. Is that a prerequisite?"

"Do you still have a thing for him?"

"A thing or two."

"Come on, do you, Sue?"

"I might, if it wouldn't make my episode with your father seem so tawdry. Not that I'm going to bring that up. Now, you. What was it Frank might've done?"

At this point the nurse parted the curtains. She had to run down to the lab, she said. Could Melissa step in for a minute? Inside, Alice was on her back, wrapped up in a sheet from shoulder to knee. "How are you?" Melissa touched her hand. At her touch, Alice squeezed her fingers, pulled on them oddly, with an almost imperceptible jerk of her head that Melissa guessed meant: Get closer. As she did, the doctor, who'd been completing paperwork on a clipboard, started, "The police—" but got no further, because the nurse returned just then with a sheaf of forms for him. "Excuse me," he said to Melissa, but before she could leave them alone Alice spoke in a hoarse voice, "No, stay."

"OK, then, if you're sure," he said. "Your pregnancy test came back positive." When the doctor had asked her if she was pregnant, Alice had not really answered. Now she reacted just as vaguely, staring back quizzically at the doctor until he was compelled to explain that this was not a consequence of the rape—the test was not effective until five days after con-ception—but it affected her options. Normally, for instance, he would offer to administer the so-called morning-after pill—and as he went on Alice pulled Melissa down close again and whispered in a tone of perplexed wonder, "Does he think they did this with a *dick*?"

"I don't know," Melissa tried to answer, but her voice didn't emerge. The doctor had stopped speaking, and Alice's insis-tent whisper filled the space. "*Oh man*," she breathed, and she started to cry.

Nobody was talking to him. They said their hellos when they passed in the hall and they stopped in, even sat down, to ask him the inevitable questions relating to business, and when they were chatting and he happened by, they went on with a nod to include him, but it wasn't the same. It was nothing he'd ever imagined he'd miss. In fact, he'd already thought, for a long time, that nobody really talked to him anyway, so to learn what it was to be truly shunned came as something of a revelation. Melissa he missed most of all, especially now that he'd come to understand what she'd stolen of his life, however unwittingly. Now that he couldn't believe that he knew more about what she was doing than she did. By the time he'd heard she was selling her house, she had sold it. The house didn't matter. He'd never cared for it, and at one time, when their father had first bought it and installed her in it and, worse yet, she'd let him, he'd actually despised it with a strength of feeling rarely leveled at a building, except perhaps for the house in which he'd grown up, and that was where she'd taken up residence with her strange ensemble. So it wasn't the house; what rankled him was how the news was already old news before it was news to him, and so clearly that his surprise caused unmistakable amusement in his slow-moving source.

She and Jesse were living on the family estate with Abel and Mrs. Carpenter and "Little" Joe Martin, who was convalescing, and, to his complete bemusement, Sue, the place taking on the character of a wartime haven for women and children and blasted men, including Alice, wounded and woman and child all at once, who wouldn't take his calls or accept his visits or even speak to him when he took the last drastic measure of intercepting her on the grounds. On spotting him, she turned and made her way back to the house, leaving him no option but to jog after her and, when that didn't work, to sneak up on her. This revealed to him the truth about his own foolishness, that he could only guess at the depths it might reach. Surprised when he spoke her name from behind, Alice screamed, summoning Little, who rocketed in his wheelchair right onto the lawn, where he sank, struggling toward them in the lush grass.

"Alice," he said, following her as she made her way to Little in his predicament, "I know what sort of impression you got from that scene at the brewery, and I know it was wrong—the impression—that's what I wanted to tell you. At least let me tell you, whatever Cole said, that business about a 'deal,' there wasn't any, no deal, nothing I knew of or would ever have condoned, never, if it meant hurting you in any way let alone—" And here he could say no more, not just because of horror at what had happened but because of the personal nature of it: in a strange way, her rape was like a pure instance of his own desire. As tormented as he was by the images of submission she'd granted him, the taunting arousal whenever they came back unbidden at a mere glimpse of her, he found it more frustrating by far to be denied her simple attention.

He could not even tell if she'd heard what he'd said. He was staring at the French braid that swung between her shoulder blades like a pendulum as she strode away, and instead of the usual pictures her reluctant presence evoked, there was visited upon him a fantastic image, bizarre in its very mundaneness, of this woman and his sister sitting crosslegged, one in front of the other, braiding each other's hair. The suspicion that he had been supplanted by an adopted "sister" was sur-

passed in its power to disturb him only by his sudden understanding that Alice had supplanted his sister as well.

It was not just the braid. It was not just her newfound ability to shun him without effort or insult. The woman was no
longer wearing the showy blue makeup. She was not wearing
makeup at all, as far as he could tell, stupid as he was on the
subject unless it was obvious, and she was wearing Melissa's
clothes. Because he'd never seen her in anything except her
uniform, and because he was as indifferent to commonplace
clothing as he was to makeup, it took him a few sightings to
see this—but Melissa did have a certain style that had subtly
registered on him over the years, as had specific garments that
he'd never been aware of noticing but which he recognized
when he saw them on Alice, whose sultry appearance assumed a peculiar innocence outfitted thus, in light cotton
things a little too big. The effect, it occurred to him with a
flicker of guilt, was like that of her uniform: a child enveloped
and all unaware her body had grown up.

She had almost reached the wheelchair and he'd almost
reached her when Jesse came bounding around the corner of
the house and, willingly or unwittingly, straight toward him.
Alice spoke his name—just that—in a cool clear voice hardly
raised, and Jesse stopped dead, then, seemingly unbidden, met
her at the wheelchair and helped turn it around. He was very
businesslike, upright as a little cadet, and only when Alice put
a hand on his shoulder did he cut a quick giddy look back at
his uncle.

For the first time since the incident, Frank went home secure in the sense that he was on his own, which, with no re-
gard to the facts of the situation, let alone his own version of
the events, suited everyone fine—and that, at the very least
and at last, was something familiar. In a way, it was like being
rid of a handicap. He was not one of their lot. He was different, of a different order, and he was unhappy. It was as if every
shaft from his father's outsize quiver had been given to

Melissa—or, God help him, to Alice—or Alice was his substitute for Melissa, and he'd traded his whole identity and the family honor for a worshipful look from an over-made-up sister he could licitly screw.

The time was propitious for him to get hold of himself. His ads—or, granted, the beer itself—had done too well, almost ruined them, and that was before the abortive lawsuit rained publicity on them. The rape had finished them. Never had Gutenbier received so much public notice, virtually all of it bad, and never had the orders been so good. It couldn't be said that he'd been wrong about the impact of women on their market. If women had stopped buying the beer in protest, nobody knew it. And he hadn't been wrong about Beeksma, who, at the least little flap, wanted out. So where had he miscalculated so badly? In not anticipating the magnitude of the new beer's success? It flattered him to think so, but didn't quite convince him. That was what had pushed the value of their stock to an unreachable height just when their resources were utterly depleted and, with the bad news and bad deal with Beeksma to consider, no bank would help them at a reasonable rate. His mistake was in not seeing where the flap would lead—who could have?—or how fast. What it came down to, ultimately, was timing.

It was in the midst of these reflections that Mike Drury of Miller, whose calls had become as regular as taxes, called again. Because of their mutual interest in Gutenbier and their mutual inability to take command of it, but most of all because he was the courted party and, short of selling out, could count on the man's deference, Frank had a certain fondness for him. He would have poured out the whole story of his plight, the peculiar bind in which he found himself and his company, if Mike Drury hadn't already known plenty about it. It was a hard thing, Mike agreed, when doing well undid you, and he recalled a story about an advertisement Rolls-Royce had run in *The New Yorker* with similar near-disastrous results, orders out of all proportion to what the company, with its painstaking approach to assembly, could fill. There was of course a parallel. Then Mike pointed out a key difference: Gutenbier had mixed up its finances with what he referred to as businessmen of principle, always a mistake, since business itself was without principles other than survival and profit. A virtuous approach to business was fine and necessary—but only with those at your mercy, not those at whose whim you might find yourself bowing and bending. "But I spoke to you back then," Mike said, somewhat hurt. "I stood ready as a fair representative of business as business to arrange just the infusion of cool cash that would see you through this, and I mean cool cash, not warm cash, sentimental or squeamish or what-have-you cash—good, clean, amoral money, and more of it where that came from, I might add, to keep those Rolls-Royces of the beer world rolling along, even in the face of devastating success."

All right, then, Frank said to him. This was clearly an opening, and what would it take to get Miller to buy Beeksma's shares—a purchase, he didn't have to add, that would immediately make them more valuable?

Go public, Mike said, and Frank laughed politely. "Make them participating," Mike suggested next, and Frank, having anticipated this, gave it a moment before he sadly concluded that this, aside from requiring the agreement of the other stockholders, who would never agree, would hopelessly skew the balance between them. But what if, and here he was ready, what if he sweetened the offer with a package of voting stock? He believed he could part with a small percentage of his own—nothing that would change the allotment of power one jot—and he might be able to pry some out of other hands, especially in view of its present value and where—he could make a convincing case that he himself didn't believe for a minute—it might be going. Would, say, 5 percent do?

He believed he had thought out every angle, every direction the talk could take, but Mike Drury surprised him, discomfited him somewhat, by readily agreeing. Immediately he looked for the variable he might have missed—and when, after long and painstaking scrutiny, none presented itself, he called his cousins, Francis and Ernest.

The next board meeting was only a few days away, and as long as everyone persisted in not talking to him, it would cost him no effort at all to keep his counsel until then.

42

Melissa discovered that she had been lonely, had been longing for company, liked nothing better than to sit at the table each morning with Sue exchanging what would've been gossip had it not concerned their intimates and immediate family. The word this morning, about Jesse, wasn't good. The assistant principal had called yesterday to say that Jesse, his friend P.J., and a girl she didn't know, named Crystal, had been caught in, as the woman had initially put it, compromising circumstances. Delicately she'd explained that the two boys, fully clothed (although there was some question about their flies) had been found in the janitor's closet with Crystal, naked but for socks and shoes, apparently conducting an anatomy lesson. The details were hopelessly blurred, because Crystal, chastened in the ensuing scandal, had cried and claimed she had been brutalized by the boys, who insisted that she'd volunteered. Melissa had asked and asked, threatening punishment, then promising none, but getting nothing out of Jesse either way.

"What's wrong with him?" she said to Sue, now that he'd gone off to the bus.

"Nothing?" Sue suggested. "He's a boy?" and then, when this failed to satisfy Melissa (or to surprise her—after all, Sue's reaction, on first hearing, had been to laugh), she said, "Didn't you ever play doctor when you were little?"

"I don't know. Maybe. When I was five or six."

"You did? With Frank?"

"I don't remember. The point is, I was—"

"What? Younger than Jesse? Innocent?"

All right, she said, OK, it was something kids did, and she didn't want to think Jesse'd done anything bad, not really, but what that girl, Crystal, had said—

Because they got caught, Sue asserted with great certainty.

Did Jesse, did Sue think, know about Alice, about—? Would he—he wouldn't—?

What? Sue said, alarmed—at the thought or her friend, it was impossible to say. Play rape? Her alarm was her answer, but she added that this was, in all likelihood, some kind of reaction to his crush on Alice, especially if he'd gotten an eyeful of her and Abel. Melissa said, Alice and Abel? Through the window she was watching him install the delphinium she'd dug up and transported from her house, the clutch of spent stalks folding over her arm like a ballerina in her death swoon, all cut back now, nothing but a wilted rosette of leaves spilling from Abel's hand.

All this was more than Melissa could absorb at once, so, after a few seconds of perplexed silence, she recalled, she brought up, one other thing that she'd meant to tell Sue, about how, in view of Jesse's multiplying and ever-more-pressing questions about his father, she'd decided to get them together. The thing was, she said, she couldn't get him. She would call, leave a message—Jim was still in Boulder—and he wouldn't call back, or she'd call and get him, or think she had until she said who she was and he claimed to be the wrong Jim, another Jim, and when she'd dial again, at once, she'd get the machine.

It had been a long time, Sue said. What did she expect?

What she'd expected was the nice, normal, uncomplicated man she'd known back then, though it was beginning to seem possible that everyone she knew would eventually turn out to be someone else, herself included, but more than anyone else her brother, who was not the man he might've been.

They were not really speaking except when absolutely necessary, so, when she found him husbanding Mike Drury around the boardroom, she resigned herself to waiting, aware that he was up to something in his way, trying to ingratiate himself but only succeeding in indicting himself further, since she knew he never made the unnecessary gesture. He was not unnecessarily subtle either, and a glance at the table, blue paper at each place, told her he'd changed the agenda, which she'd had copied on white. Instinctively she looked around for Curtis, who was just walking in, sat down beside her, squeezed her hand under the table. Reinforced, she took up the agenda and discovered that Mike Drury was now her colleague—or, more accurately, his enormous company, invested in his nice neat person, was. And with that she commenced the meeting, whose first order of business was Frank's account of their precarious finances, the pretext, apparently, for Drury's presence. It all did seem to work out, though Frank's perfectly reasonable answers to her questions and Curtis's did little to convince her that the move itself was perfectly reasonable.

She delivered her own discomfiting news, which Frank of course knew at least as well as she did: The orders were beginning, just beginning, to go down—as they did every September, and yet she feared a high rate of returns now that the bounce they'd gotten from the publicity was subsiding. Where was the advantage of all the business they'd done, all the improvements, if they couldn't keep up with demand and when demand lulled there was no money left to pay for the improvements? Speaking, she looked at Curtis, at Drury, at Henry and Martin, Ernest and Francis (and if they'd sold their shares, what were they doing here? It seemed impolite to ask), only glancingly at Frank, the one she was addressing through the others, as in a court where there was no directly approaching the royal person, though who that would be here, she or her brother, she couldn't say.

"I'd like to suggest something," he was saying, with a casual disregard for protocol. "I touched on it once, but, in view of the way things are going right now, it's become somewhat urgent—you yourself just said as much"—this to Melissa. What he proposed was what he'd proposed before, but without any allowance for Melissa's continued role: a shifting of their positions to appease potential lenders. "For the company's sake, but yours too," he said, "because of the link everyone'll be making, rightly or wrongly, between your command and the troubles we've had—"

"In which you aren't implicated, is that right?" Curtis said.

"I'm as responsible as anyone—that's a given—in the same way you"—he spoke to her, not Curtis—"you're behind all the improvements we've made, the expansion, upgrades, new product—but because I *initiated* them, saw them along, and so forth, they look like my work, at least enough so that if I were to assume control maybe we could finagle a deal. Whereas right now . . ." His eyebrows, arching across the ellipsis, said everything about the uncertainty of their situation. "It's the company I'm concerned about."

"What else?" The question came from Curtis.

"Excuse me?"

"What else would you be concerned about?"

"Curtis, it might surprise you, but my sister's position and reputation mean something to me."

"Surprise me? Not at all, in view of the lengths you've gone to to damage them."

Frank looked genuinely startled, as if that scene with Cole and Hauser, which she'd related to Curtis, were nothing but the men's mutual hallucination—as it truly must seem to him, she concluded, knowing his face as she did. "Excuse *me*," she said, and, not wanting to check the stirring at her side, got the disconcerting feeling that she'd surprised Curtis as much as her brother. "Let me get this straight. It's hard for me, you know, I get so confused. You arrange financing that brings us to the edge of bankruptcy, conceive a marketing scheme that, along with your special handling of personnel policy, almost lands us in federal court, earns us unpleasant publicity, and influences a vicious attack on one of our employees, which is exactly what fudges the already suspect financial deal you engineered—and *I'm* the liability when we go to the bank?"

"I've done everything I could to ease you in the right direction, Melissa, but I couldn't make up for—" Frank took a sharp breath, implying a powerful act of self-restraint. "You came to the job with certain handicaps, having come to it late. And I know your loyalties are unbudgeable." As if thinking better of the route he was taking, he tacked abruptly: "The long and short of it is, you've been in charge. Whatever I've done, I've done from a subordinate position."

"Then I see no reason we shouldn't vote on your proposal," she said as coolly as she could.

"If we do, then I'd like Curtis to excuse himself, in view of his personal stake in the outcome."

All the restraint she'd marshaled to keep from erupting was gathered now at the base of her throat, and she knew she was flushing. She managed to speak in a level voice: "Whatever you mean—" but Curtis cut in, sounding as calm as she wished to appear, "Frank, I don't see how I could possibly have a more personal stake in this business than you or Melissa."

There was a conclusive curtness to this, but Frank was not finished, simply waited him out with a curious look, then explained patiently, "It would seem to complicate things that you're sleeping with my sister, that is to say, your colleague, client, and junior by—what is it?—twenty years, or is it only eighteen?"

She was choking. She could hear the blood in her ears, her thunderous pulse, and beyond that the silence, the stillness, like a storm about to break, one vast caught breath. She examined her hands, folded there on the table, and felt Curtis shift.

"First of all," she said almost under her breath, trying to

steady her voice, "whatever relationship I have with Curtis is none of your business, let alone the business of anyone else here. Second, what's suspect isn't my relationship with *Curtis*. It's my relationship with *you*, because, if I weren't your sister, if my sisterly sympathy and compassion hadn't clouded my vision, then I would've seen the obvious flaws in every move you made, every policy I let you bully through. I would've seen the repercussions we're seeing now, all the damage that's starting to look irreparable—so not only will we cease to be Gutenbier, which seems exactly what you've had in mind, we'll cease to be. Not that there's any difference. But you don't see it. We're not Miller Brewing. If we stop being Gutenbier, we're nothing. Don't you see it? Don't you think that might be why our father left me in charge? Because—and maybe it's just *egomania*—because he didn't want his life's work to just disappear?"

"You don't know what you're saying, Melissa. Everything's fine."

This did stop her for a second, fury giving way to incredulity. "Fine?" she demanded. "How can you say *fine*? After what happened to Alice. Because of *you*."

"*You*," he said. "Because of *you*. Your presence. The resentment you caused, when all anyone really wanted was continuity."

"Me?" His interpretation had become so absurd, she could feel her disbelief, could hear it in her tone, rising into the range of hysteria. With an effort, determined he wouldn't find further proof of his point in this public exchange, she spoke evenly, "Was it me who gave those thugs, Cole and Hauser, the impression, rightly or wrongly, that anything they could do to upset things, *any*thing, even attack . . . a woman who . . . it would somehow serve the company's interests in the end?"

Luckily, because she had been so close to saying something about Alice's condition, which seemed for an instant like certain evidence of Frank's perfidy, Curtis intervened to say that, in view of the circumstances, perhaps the most sensible thing would be to go ahead with the vote Melissa had proposed.

"And as to your participation?" Frank said. "Tainted as it is."

"*His* vote is tainted?" she burst out. "At least when *he's* screwing me I know it."

Apparently this was so vulgar that Frank couldn't immediately frame a response—or do anything but stare at her, until he said quietly, "Then I guess you know about the deal he made with Jesse's father? Of course—what else would keep a man away from you for twelve years? Let alone his son? What else, but more money than some good old-fashioned contact would've gotten him, good old regular Jim—except good old regular Jim's not so regular now—is he, Curtis? He's almost rich enough for Princess Melissa, the only catch being, he can't even see her or he'll be his poor old unsuitable self again. But Curtis was only the go-between—unless it was all his idea—who ever knew, with Tweedledee and Tweedledum? And it's all the same when it comes to this *screwing* metaphor, isn't it? So we can say with relative accuracy: Our father's still screwing you, Mel. Screwing you, screwing with you, it's all the same—don't you think he foresaw this? Do you really imagine that he saw you running the company that was his whole life? And mine? You, who can't even manage an affair, let alone a household? No, this was exactly what he had in mind. I know it. I knew him. Better than you. Because I had to. And I could've protected you from all of this. None of it had to happen—if you'd just been willing to show me a *fraction* of the respect I deserved, I'd *earned*, while you were trashing everything you got without trying. But you had to have everything. You had to. Now you have it, Melissa. How does it feel?"

She found herself standing. She said, not waiting out the tremor in her voice this time, "I don't see any reason to pursue the vote now that we all know how it would go. In fact, I think we should adjourn this meeting and reconvene in a week."

"Move to adjourn, reconvene in a week," Ernest pronounced solemnly, and no one objected that he was no longer eligible to do so.

When no second seemed forthcoming, Mike Drury raised his hand halfway and put forth, like a tentative suggestion, "Second?"

They were saying their "ayes," all watching her, as she turned to go. Her glance only grazed Curtis, who hadn't the nerve to stop her, or even leap up and follow her any faster than he would have anyway—she heard it, the pause, the dignified gathering of himself to stand, nod to the others as, under the shuffling, the subdued movements and scraping of chairs, the door inched closed, and she found herself alone in the hallway with Mike Drury.

PART FOUR

43

What was bred as proprietary in the father was borne out in the son as stewardship, in the daughter as belonging. Of ownership, he'd passed on only instruments and documents, which could be negotiated, and as of the next meeting, convened a week later by Drury, the Johnson family ownership of Gutenbier was a thing of the past. Frank retained his share of the company, and his was the only position that remained the same, but he felt the change more than anyone else; Curtis, there to be released as counsel, could see it in the way he sat, pale and still, almost psychotically attentive, like a boy hoping against all probability that his chastened demeanor might persuade his elders of the redundancy of punishment. Curtis began to feel a suspicion of pity for the man. From there it was not far to wondering whether he might have allied himself with Frank rather than Melissa, to better effect—better, even if this denouement was exactly what Francis had in mind, the penchant for control outlasting a man only in negative fashion, in whatever sadistic form. The idea didn't last a minute, started to collapse as soon as he saw where it led, Melissa pandered to him by her father, although he was reminded of a moment, one he had put down to the perversities of grief, when, sorting through his dead wife's things, Francis had commented, "I always thought you and Maria would have made a pretty pair." It was also true that Francis, with his predilection for spreading his interests, liked not so much to share as to confer, displaying to the best effect his power to do so. Curtis drew back from this too, not liking himself in its light any more than he might like Francis were he to keep this up, a search that turned up every hidden thing except its object.

What was missing was Melissa. On that, he and Frank could agree. She had eluded them both. Holed up in her compound with all manner of impromptu security—impenetrable unless one was prepared to rush a man in a wheelchair or to make that reporter do what she was told or to bribe a boy of eleven—she had left them to speculate, becoming finally like her father, invisible cynosure that he was.

So it was that he found himself, sometime later, approaching Frank in the Greenleaf, where he was sitting alone drinking Gutenbier Light from the bottle, a folded newspaper under his hand. He raised the bottle to Curtis in a toast: "Soon to be a collector's item."

"A few too many on the market, I'm afraid. May I?" He was warily allowed. Two tables away was Lillian, with a man wearing a neck brace. Taking his seat, Curtis nodded uncomfortably.

"I've done you a disservice, Frank," he said when the waitress had come and gone. "I've started to wonder if I haven't had everything absolutely backward almost from the first. All along I thought it was your father who understood you all too well. It was a vision I deferred to, I admit."

"What're you saying, Curtis?" Frank was brusque.

"I'm saying, you seem to have understood him well enough yourself. And it occurs to me that that could have colored, could have blackened, his opinion. Which became my opinion. Wrongly, I warrant."

Frank considered him with a sober fascination. Then he said, "You worm. Wasn't it enough to fuck my sister, now you want me too?"

Curtis said, "I hardly—"

" 'Hardly'?" He laughed. "You haven't got a distant clue

about what my father thought. What he knew. You never had a prayer. You could read his books and listen to his music and lust after his wife and sink yourself up to the ears in his company and never even touch the thing, the quick, the thing that made you want to." Curtis's sadness slowly opened, blossomed through him hot and pungent like a powerful liquor. Much as he missed Melissa, much as missing a woman had its practical, immediate pangs, it began to seem possible that she was merely a stop on the way to real grief, begun like a glimpse of something inescapably vast and empty upon Francis's death. He *was* a worm. The revelation wasn't surprising, in fact brought with it the brief comfort of certainty, and he regarded Frank gravely, intently, intent upon knowing, perhaps for the last time, his place.

44

It was what he'd wanted, only more so, and if he'd had to be half killed to get it, so be it. Finally walking again, he went off to work, where he was a hero and where he hardly had to work at all. Instead he had only to make an appearance, start to lift a pallet or adjust a hose, check a meter, take a spell at the Filtec, all to the welcoming smiles and a momentary turn in the talk of the other workers, a routine that it struck him must be very like what it was to go senile or nutty in a big, tolerant family. If not for the last frayed shred of his belief that work was what kept him going, he wouldn't have gone at all. It was what gave him purpose and his days structure, or so he'd thought from the start of his first real job, or so he seemed to remember thinking. But now he discovered he could do well enough, would not go to pieces or wander directionless without it, as long as he had money, as long as he was, as they said, set. And suddenly he was.

He had a kid too now, ready-made, already old enough to play ball, and an ace pitcher to boot. He and Jesse were shagging balls in the yard. Because he wasn't yet completely steady in the eyes of the medical profession and women, who were perpetually monitoring his outdoor activity for risky maneuvers like diving for flies, Sue was backing him up, and now she shouted from behind him, "OK, Jesse, have you done your homework?"

Jesse answered, "Hunh?" as if he hadn't heard. Little roughed the kid up on their way to the house, mussed his hair, kneaded his shoulders, traded body checks. At the door they both became dignified, as befitted the men of the house.

He was going to have a kid of his own too, a girl, they thought, though Alice explained that all babies began as girls. Lately a pregnancy expert, she could talk about zygotes and ultrasounds and transition, which was a technical expression, he was happy to hear. She and Melissa were in the den, sitting on the sofa watching TV, Melissa with a magazine open on her lap. She patted the space between her and Alice. They were watching one of their shows, and Alice was filling him in on the progress Melissa was making with Jesse's father (to which he listened only halfheartedly, believing that a father whose attentions could be bought off was no father at all), when a picture of a bottle of Gutenbier came on the screen. Alice squeaked. Everyone fell silent. The bottle wasn't like the ones he handled every day at work. It was squatter and darker, and the label looked like something printed by hand. The little book-and-bottle logo was still there, though, at the corner of the name, like a registered-trademark symbol. Above the bottle were the words: *In the spirit of the ages.* A page of antique script scrolled past as a rolling bass voice said, "George Washington took his recipe with him when he went to war. James Madison and Thomas Jefferson conferred on the merits of brewing methods." It went on, "The Commonwealth of Massachusetts passed an act to encourage its manufacture and consumption." Another page appeared, with the camera closing in on a passage that a different, distant, sonorous voice read: "And whereas the wholesome qualities of malt liquors greatly recommend them to general use, as an important means of preserving the health of the citizens of this Commonwealth . . . ," fading near the end.

"Who are we to disagree?" the original voice asked.

"Gutenbier," the deep voice intoned as the old bottle reappeared, then transformed into a new one—and it was the new one, redesigned to look something like the old. "It's good for the country. It's good for you. And . . . it's good." Under the bottle a printed parting line appeared—"It's pasteurized"— which got a laugh from Sue.

Little could tell without looking that no one was looking at Melissa. Gutenbier was like her brother or her father, an absence nobody spoke of, out of deference to her although she'd never asked them not to. He would rather have been wrong than hurt her feelings, so he went along, but he didn't quite believe the reasoning behind it all, because, sad as she seemed sometimes, Melissa didn't strike him as the type to overlook the obvious, no matter how willing everyone else was to do so in her behalf.

She settled back on the couch, a rustle of warmth at his shoulder, and flicked her hand at the television as if she'd just made a point. Everybody waited, but Melissa didn't say anything. Lying back, she turned her head his way. He felt it as a breath and cautiously turned too, but couldn't tell if she was looking at him, over him, at Alice, at them both, at no one in particular, or at everyone. He turned the other way, to Alice, who took a second out from the show to smile at him too, a smile that barely touched him before she returned to the television, which she looked at just as she'd looked at him and had looked at him months ago and years ago, always with the illusion of looking up, anticipating something, lips parted a little in that way that had once seemed so suggestive but now, no different, merely because of the baby, seemed more like the look of Mary waiting on her angel. There was no way of telling, no way of knowing, other than a certain feeling, what it meant, what either of them, any of them, ever meant, but between the two of them, bit by bit, he was coming to believe this wasn't too much mystery for a man to bear.

A NOTE ON THE TYPE

The text of this book was set in Times Ten, a version of a typeface called Times New Roman, originally designed by Stanley Morison (1889–1967) for The Times (London) and first introduced by that newspaper in 1932.

Among typographers and designers of the twentieth century, Stanley Morison was a strong forming influence—as a typographical adviser to the Monotype Corporation, as a director of two distinguished publishing houses, and as a writer of sensibility, erudition, and keen practical sense.

Composed by Dix,
Syracuse, New York

Printed and bound by The Haddon Craftsmen,
an R. R. Donnelley & Sons Company,
Bloomsburg, Pennsylvania

Designed by Iris Weinstein